I've travelled the world twice over,
Met the famous: saints and sinners,
Poets and artists, kings and queens,
Old stars and hopeful beginners,
I've been where no-one's been before,
Learned secrets from writers and cooks
All with one library ticket
To the wonderful world of books.

ABERCROMBIE'S AUNT
And Other Stories

In this splendid assortment of tales, Jan Webster watches keenly for the fatal word or gesture that can alter a life or relationship forever. From career women sighing over the men who got away; the steady men of Jonquil Close trying to keep a rein on their wives now that they have returned to work; to Jean, Abercrombie's aunt who comes from Scotland laden with cake and criticism. Here are twelve stories that are guaranteed to raise a smile.

Books by Jan Webster
in the Ulverscroft Large Print Series:

COLLIERS ROW
SATURDAY CITY
BEGGARMAN'S COUNTRY
DUE SOUTH
MUCKLE ANNIE
ONE LITTLE ROOM
A DIFFERENT WOMAN
I CAN ONLY DANCE WITH YOU
BLUEBELL BLUE

JAN WEBSTER

◆

ABERCROMBIE'S AUNT

And Other Stories

Complete and Unabridged

ULVERSCROFT
Leicester

First published in Great Britain in 1990 by
Robert Hale Limited
London

First Large Print Edition
published November 1992
by arrangement with
Robert Hale Limited
London

British Library CIP Data

Webster, Jan
Abercrombie's aunt and other stories.
—Large print ed.—
Ulverscroft large print series: general fiction
I. Title
823.914 [FS]

ISBN 0–7089–2760–2

Published by
F. A. Thorpe (Publishing) Ltd.
Anstey, Leicestershire
Set by Words & Graphics Ltd.
Anstey, Leicestershire
Printed and bound in Great Britain by
T. J. Press (Padstow) Ltd., Padstow, Cornwall

Abercrombie's Aunt, Abercrombie's Wedding and *Back Payments* all made their first appearance in *Punch*. *Rose Would Be A Lovely Name For It* appeared in the Arts Council's *New Stories 1*.

Contents

1 Bits of Burt Reynolds 1
2 Abercrombie's Aunt 27
3 A Kindness 44
4 Rose Would Be A
   Lovely Name For It 65
5 Abercrombie's Wedding 98
6 Starter Homes 114
7 Back Payments 129
8 Sweet Milk Scone
   Meets Godzilla 146
9 Abercrombie and the
   Dodgy Situation 166
10 Something Sportive 182
11 Going to See Pavlova 206
12 Over the Hill 218

1

Bits of Burt Reynolds

THE girls had got there early and taken the prime seat in the corner window of the pub restaurant. I say girls for women are girls forever these days. It was an up-market establishment in this frisky Northern town and Management (Mrs Evelyn Ducksworth) had resisted nothing in the name of good taste when it came to festoon blinds, silk tassles for the peach curtains, brass lamps, carved balustrades, stiff tablecloths, scalloped napkins, gilt-framed prints a long way after Constable and Renoir and flourished capitals on the fat menu cards. The effect, Gina said, was a bit Edwardian, opulent and redolent of high-kicking good times. The food was lavish and well cooked. They knew this, for these days they made something of a fetish of eating out.

The girls relaxed before noon on

the padded velvet banquettes, letting the sense of good living, of very slight naughtiness or risqueness seep through their well maintained bodies. Car salesmen in sharp pale suits came here, businessmen with Porsches and sweating eager faces, as well as the County *haut monde* connected with advertising sport and the media. Occasionally the changing boyish laugh of a well-known telly presenter boomed off the polished tankards. Intermingled were self-conscious pensioners being taken out for birthday treats, Mum's white hair twisted into clean tight curls, family parties, trendy younger mums defiantly shoving red-faced protesting babies into the smart high-chairs provided, refusing to be left at home as *their* mothers had, out of all the fun. It was very popular. It gave value for money and the waitresses were nice to deaf old aunties and those who took a long time to make up their minds. The Muzak played waltzes and low mellow Johnny Mathis.

"We'll go there," Velma had insisted, when Gina's birthday had started looming. "It'll be my treat. We'll go through the menu, girl. No holds barred."

Normally as they both worked as personal secretaries to captains of industry lunch would have been a wholemeal sandwich, two wedges of tomato and a smattering of Iceberg. But Velma had detected a slight need for cheering up and had arranged for their days off to synchronise. Gina got down a little more often these days. She had this moping unsubstantiated thing for a divorced doctor newly come to the town and although Velma could not see it ever coming to anything, her friend clung on to the buoy-rope of hope. "He definitely *looked* at me when we met in the bookshop," she said. "With his eyes. There was a kind of frisson." Frisson-smeethong, Velma thought. People said the daftest things when they were smitten.

Since it was to be an occasion, there had been a lot of deliberation over what to wear, exploratory visits to boutiques in Wilmslow, Bramhall and Sale. Consultations as to whether knitted suits purchased only a few months ago might do, with a new blouse, or whether the amethyst had been a mistake in Velma's case, making her look washed-out, just as possibly that vivid green had run its course too memorably soon with Gina. They were comfortably off, independent women and could afford to spend on clothes, but they had to square it with conscience first. You had to look smart but you must never go completely over the top, as Velma maintained. There were those children in Ethiopia.

In the end the birthday girl had indulged in a Marcelle Griffon because it was kind to her hips and you could go anywhere in navy and Velma had bought new eyeshadow that helped her to look less sallow and they both knew they were looking pretty damn good for forty-blah. They had never given in, even when Gina's husband had died only three years after their marriage and Velma had had to give Rotten Donald his divorce. Gina had attended Stretchexcise classes six weeks after the funeral. Chin up had been the motto and after a while it became statutory. Look good and you feel good was their credo and modern women these days did not need to depend on men. Much.

Gina had a pleasant flat in a converted house and a white Fiesta car and Velma had a cottage to satisfy her artistic side and an Alfa-Romeo of uncertain age and temperament because, she said, it looked ropey and louche and she had a perverse kind of pleasure in driving something no one expected her to drive.

You are funny about cars, was Gina's comment. She looked suspiciously at her friend, wondering if there was more to Velma's nature than she let on.

Management (Mrs Evelyn Ducksworth) gave the occasion her imprimatur by coming up to them with the menu herself. Velma had not quite pigeon-holed her as yet. With her slim figure, always clad in black or grey, she could pass for twenty-eight in a good light, but the dark, knowing eyes spoke experience, disillusion even. Allied to a laugh that had known smoky bars, pillows impermanently dented next to Mrs Ducksworth's sleek dark head, promises like piecrust, the eyes said customers were always welcome, friendly overtures less so.

"Special occasion, ladies, is it?" enquired Mrs Ducksworth, pencil at the ready.

"It is my friend here's birthday," said Velma. "And we are going through the card. What do you think, Evelyn?" she asked, with rash familiarity, but it was their fourth time there and they had already had the daiquiris.

"The sole bonne femme? The tornedos Rossini? Everything's good." Mrs Ducksworth loved food. It was what made her good at her job.

The birthday girl gazed at her over the rim of her menu. Gina's eyes had glazed already, ever so slightly, from the strength of the drinks. Mrs Ducksworth noted how her pale blonde hair had been carefully set and tousled, how the mauve eye-shadow had been fastidiously applied and make-up pressed into the fine cracks around her eyes and mouth and how the face, set in a determination to enjoy, still looked somehow pinched and, you had to say it, deprived.

"Have the duck," she suggested, impulsively. "And maybe the coquilles Saint-Jacques to start." She had been known to hold these back for the Roller owners coming in from Manchester. In spite of herself, she found herself asking Gina, "Did you get some nice presents? For the birthday? What you wanted?"

Velma shrieked. "She wanted Burt Reynolds, really, but she didn't get him."

"I got flowers," said Gina. "Scent. Things like that."

"We'll have champagne," Velma decided. "Moët et Chandon." At Gina's restraining look she patted her friend's hand. "No, no. We're having a day out. We've waited for this." She waved a hand at Mrs Evelyn Ducksworth. "Yes, bring the duck. And the coquille Saint Whatsit. That will do nicely." She had the impression people were looking at them and subsided back in her chair. "That was all right, wasn't it?" she demanded of Gina. Her friend nodded. Sometimes it was easier just to give Velma her head.

"I had a card from that fellow," said Gina.

"What fellow?"

"You know, the one who followed us around in Rimini. Jack Spalding."

"How did he know?"

"He remembered from last year. That's

where we were. On my birthday. In Rimini."

"You could have made a conquest there. I always said."

"You what? He had a handshake like a wet fish. He would have talked car exhausts till the cows came home. That's what he travelled in."

"What?"

"Car exhausts."

"Must have been damned uncomfortable." Velma gave a hoot. When she had two daiquiris she made this noise like a drunken owl.

"Look," said Gina lightly, "watch it, Tootsie. We don't want to end up under the table. Even if it is my birthday."

She was aware of the tension in an elderly couple at a table nearby, caused by their trying very hard not to look in their direction. "Velma," she said more severely, "be your age. Don't drink any more till the food comes."

"I don't feel my age," said Velma defiantly. "Do you? Do you feel your age? I am still seventeen. Nineteen at the most. And I always will be. Nineteen inside."

"I was nineteen when I met my husband, Ian," said Gina.

"You're not going to get all misty on me, are you?"

Gina's mouth tightened minimally. "What do you mean? I don't. I don't get misty. I must ask you to remember I was widowed. It is different. There was none of the bitterness that comes from divorce, Velma."

"I'm not bitter."

"At times you are. Twitter and bisted." Gina smiled at her friend to take the sting from her words.

"I would only like to disembowel him. If I ever meet him again."

"Remember this is a time of celebration, Velma. You said. Not a time for recrimination."

"OK. Go on about Ian if you like. You will, anyhow."

"Dr Smallwood — Colin — reminds me of him."

"How can he? Ian was a builder and had shoulders like a tank. The doc wears sandals and eats scented cachous."

"That's not true about the cachous. Well, only the once. Because he'd had

9

a small sherry from a grateful patient's mother."

Velma gazed at her friend in some exasperation.

"He's never once asked you out, has he? What are you building your hopes on?"

"He wouldn't. Ask me out. Not straight away. Because he's been hurt. He's still getting over the divorce. You should know all about that. But there is a sort of rapport between us. He's aware of it as well as me. We both like painting water-colours, we both take the *Amateur Painter* — that's what we spoke about in the bookshop — and he likes string quartets and so do I."

"How do you know? Did he tell you?"

"He was buying tickets for the concert at the Hall."

"Oh, well, maybe . . . " Velma conceded reluctantly. "But I don't want you getting down if things don't develop. Look, you have a beautiful home. You've just taken delivery of an antique desk and a duck-feather duvet. There's a Handel rose going up your wall I'd give my eye teeth for, and you can sit out on the

10

patio without being overseen. Romance needn't come into it. Isn't that what we've said?"

"But a life can be very lonely without sex, Velma."

"Sex, is it now? Just the pure mechanics, you mean? I thought we were talking meeting of true minds."

"True sex should include that. That's why the Jack Spaldings don't rate, even if they do send cards with messages."

"What messages?"

"I'm not telling."

Mrs Evelyn Ducksworth appeared at the table, bearing the coquilles Saint-Jacques and behind her, the wine waiter made a show of taking the champagne from its bucket and popping the cork.

"Now then," said Mrs Evelyn Ducksworth, fixing Gina with an eye. "You can't have Burt Reynolds, but you will enjoy the scallops, I guarantee. *Bon appetit!*"

Velma held her champagne glass towards her friend. Thank goodness, she thought, she's perking up a bit. She was remembering her hysterectomy three years ago. Gina coming down the ward with her arm full of pink carnations and *Homes and Gardens* for her. And, if you like, the time her mortgage had been held up and Gina had allowed her to stow her bits and pieces all over the immaculate flat, with its Doulton and ribbon-plates and Laura Ashley cushions. They'd seen each other pale-faced and depressed, in washed-out dressing-gowns when illness struck and defiant in the face of domestic crises like chimneys that fell down and washing-machines that flooded. At times Velma could scream at Gina but she was the best and sometimes the only friend she'd got.

"Your friend's birthday?" queried the lady pensioner at the table for two, having got over her previous shyness now her sherry had gone down.

Velma nodded. A family party heard the exchange and the uncle who was being the life and soul conducted any lunchers who wished to join in singing "Happy Birthday to You." Gina blushed, but the champagne was chilled and delicious. She took generous gulps, feeling the bubbles leap through her like little darting fish and when she looked up and round the pub it looked different, sunny, deliquescent, full of smiling, approving faces.

"They say the British are cold and unfeeling," commented Velma. The duck had arrived and was meltingly good. With a flourish Mrs Evelyn Ducksworth placed the vegetables on the table. "Morning gathered," she announced, and the buttered sliced courgettes, the string beans, the serrated carrots dusted with parsley, glistened happily under the sunburst of her approval. "English people can be as warm as the next," said Velma. "They all want you to have a great birthday. Aren't you glad you came?"

When she looked up from a mouthful of duck and orange, Gina was looking at her with her mouth working.

"You're never going to strike?" demanded Velma, appalled, and using the old working-class word deliberately, to deflect. Gina hated it when she betrayed her origins, saying certain expressions were just too common to be encouraged. But it didn't work this time: two tears appeared like large glistening orbs at the side of Gina's eyes and slid with a certain slow easy elegance down her cheeks.

"I'm just so happy," said Gina into her handkerchief. "As you rightly say, Velma, I have so much. The flat, the car, a holiday to look forward to. And all this. The duck is out of this world."

"Good." Velma poured some more champagne.

"At such times, I think Ian is looking down at me, saying yes, go on, enjoy yourself. He would have enjoyed this meal, especially the scallops. He liked anything seafoody."

"He liked anything foody. Let's face it, dear, he was a hedonist."

"But he had soul, Velma. Ian had soul."

"And he gave you a good time in bed."

"Velma!"

"Ooh-hoo!" cried Velma. "Don't let's beat about the bush. That's what matters. My Donald never hackled himself together in that respect. He was a rotten bloody lover."

"Vel-MA!"

"We went to marriage guidance. They told me he found me threatening. Can you believe it?"

"You never said that before."

"Why else would he go off with an 18-year-old bimbo?"

Gina gazed across the peach tablecloth at her friend, moving a frond of fern that was in with the carnations the better to see her face. Her own complexion had become quite hectically pink. Her eyeshadow had smudged somewhat from the tears and there were traces of melted butter on her upper lip. Velma looked . . . it was hard to describe how she looked. As though some further world-shaking confidence was about to burst forth from her. As though something she had kept buttoned up inside wanted to spiral from her in an ugly, crooked flowering.

"Have some more champagne," suggested Gina, timorously.

"'sfinished," said Velma. "We'll have cognac with the coffees."

"But first the sweet, Velma. Then you were going to tell me about this new health club you're thinking of joining."

"I've got to do something to shift the flab. Trouble is I have this hobby."

"What's that?"

15

"Eating."

Mrs Evelyn Ducksworth appeared again with the menu. "Would you like to choose from the trolley, ladies? Or what about one of our special ice-cream sundaes? Banana split, strawberry coupe . . . We even have a birthday special."

"What is in that?" demanded Velma.

"It's a secret," said the landlady, with a mischievous smile. "But I can recommend it."

"We'll have it," said Gina, "and blow our waistlines. They've gone already."

"That's the spirit," said Mrs Evelyn Ducksworth.

"And coffee and cognac to follow," said Velma. "Double cognac. 'sall right. We've got a taxi coming."

The ices, when they came, were a triumph of the confectioner's art. Totally over the top. Strawberry, coffee, vanilla were doused in raspberry *coulis*, dotted with pear, peach and strawberry, crowned with whipped cream and a cherry, finished off with a fantail wafer. And the landlady had set off two sparklers in each. The sight was so glorious the pensioners at the table for two burst into

16

spontaneous applause, the lady pensioner and her husband having shared a rather good bottle of Mouton Cadet by now on top of the sherries.

Mrs Evelyn Ducksworth fastened Gina, the birthday girl, with a ribald yet distant eye. "There may even be bits of Burt Reynolds in there," she said, "but which bits I am not at liberty to say.

"Oooh-hoo!" cried Velma. "Ooh-hoo! Evelyn, you are a one! I'm not coming back here. I'm too good for this place." A gentleman from Leeds had just come in from the car park in search of onion soup and a steak and was observing the girls approvingly from the bar. "Ooh-hoo!" cried Velma. "Don't look now but I think he fancies me."

Quivers of apprehension chased themselves across Gina's face. She had a feeling something was getting out of hand but the processes of her mind were slowing up somewhat and she could not quite sort out what she should be saying or doing.

"I need to go to the loo," she announced and rose a little unsteadily, holding her handbag in front of her like a chamber-pot.

In the salubrious toilets she took in the thoughtful touches that raised this establishment out of the common ruck — the hand cream, the pastel tissues, the freshener pads for the face, the dried flowers arranged in the dainty baskets, and felt a little reassured.

The only thing about going out with Velma was this tendency to get — what was that word the tabloids used? — raunchy. Gina's mother wouldn't have liked it and although she was tidily laid to rest her word still counted. Gina dashed cold water on her face, but it didn't help much. She was remembering that her mother hadn't liked Ian either and had spiked the idea of their marriage for all of six years. Six years they might have had together. When they might have had a child. All because her mother hadn't liked the sound of Ian's vowels or been able to forgive him for coming to see her once in his overalls. What a snob her mother had been. Gina glared at her own face in the mirror as though it were her parent's. A wish that Ian could materialise, just for a moment or two, hold her, kiss her, became so powerful she almost staggered. Ian metamorphosed into Colin Smallwood and she briefly ran their latest encounter over in her mind. She felt the need. It was no good Velma saying men could be discounted. Velma had made a distinct play for that gambling vicar in Rimini and sundry other males on that cruise they'd gone on together. Velma couldn't talk. Had she really made that moaning sound just now? Corks, what if somebody had come in? They could have got to hear about it at Belford and Wilderswood and her boss was already getting shirty about her tendency to wool-gather on occasion.

Oh Gina Paterwood, Gina Paterwood, she reproached herself, this is what happens when you look upon the wine when it is red. Or white. Or Champagne. Pull yourself together. But she wasn't skeins of thread, or string. She was a slippery, slithery, amorphous, evasive, disintegrating, near-menopausal female and look! in the mirror there, her skirt hem was unravelling and the bow on her new blouse was all wrong. All wrong! She wept vexatious tears as she tried to right it and then fought with her hair to get it to look worth the preposterous amount of money she had spent on it. It was no bloody use. She was a mess and nothing brought Ian back. When you were gone you were gone.

She took a series of deep breaths as she'd been taught at her relaxation classes and bashed her way back through the toilet door and the by now busy bar to the restaurant.

The man in the phosphorescent suit, who had sought onion soup, was now seated on the chair opposite Velma. He held out his hand to Gina and said ingratiatingly "I hope you have a lovely birthday." She knew then he sold burglar alarms or double glazing, for he was good at being nice to people he didn't give a hoot for, really, and he would rather have Velma to himself. As for Velma, there was no need for her to look quite so pleased with herself. A few words in a pub buttered no parsnips. Feeling sour and vinegary, Gina tucked herself into the corner of the banquette and sipped her brandy. She would opt out of the conversation. It was banal in the extreme, anyhow, about how you got to Worksop via Chesterfield and an out-of-the-way cafe that did Bakewell tart. Velma never read, of course. Magazines, yes, books no. She just carried them around with her and never knew the plot.

With Colin Smallwood, now, Gina felt sure you would be able to talk about the serials on BBC2 and even vouchsafe the fact that you occasionally wrote a line or two of poetry. He might be that way inclined himself. It was his sensitivity that attracted her. The fact that he didn't raise his voice. She would be prepared to put up with the slight curvature. Not like the men who were obviously Velma's cup of tea. So bloody cocksure and red-faced and laying down routes over the Peak as though they were Holy Writ. Gina took another sip of brandy, slipping into a not unpleasant kind of reverie where Colin Smallwood had his arm around her shoulder and was leading her down into bluebell woods, quoting Housman . . .

"Gina." Velma's voice clanged and reverberated in her ear. "Time to go, lovie. Party's over."

Gina shook herself like a cat. "Heavens to Betsy," she remonstrated, "*I* was nearly over. Asleep."

"You've dropped your handbag," said Velma. "Ooh-hoo."

"Let me help," said the onion-soup lover, whose name apparently was Graham. They all went down on one knee, picking up lipstick, solid perfume, keys and to Gina's eternal embarrassment, a packet of Dr White's.

Gina crashed into the sweet trolley as she rose and Mrs Evelyn Ducksworth's valedictory smile turned to one of strained patience. "I can't seem to," said Gina, and again "I can't seem to," but it was difficult to remember, for a few seconds, what she couldn't seem to. Stand up, it appeared. Onion Soup and Velma took up position on either side of her, putting their arms around her waist and propping her up.

"She's had more than she ought," said Velma, treacherously.

In the circumstances, it was a preposterous thing for Velma to say. Gina fought off her friend strenuously, aggrievedly. In the struggle, she dropped her handbag again and Mrs Evelyn Ducksworth's pupils hit the ceiling. Gina felt first the hook and then the zipper go on her skirt and the silky lining slooped and drooped. The tie of her blouse was undone again. She tried to put everything right at once and was suddenly hit between the eyes by a blinding pain.

"Come on, old girl, you're fine." Graham the onion-soup lover looked into her face reassuringly. He wasn't so bad close to: kindly of eye, non-judgemental. In some ways she preferred him, infinitely, to traitorous Velma, who stood there as though she weren't tanked up too and had just stepped out of the proverbial bandbox.

Gina put a hand to her skirt to hold it up. Velma had shoved her handbag with its restored contents under her arm. Her supporters urged her out of the pub before any further catastrophe struck. Gina began to weep at the humiliation of it all. A birthday, up the spout, and each one getting nearer the fifty mark. And she had never, ever, been under the weather the way she was now.

She saw the taxi they had hired at the far side of the car park, the driver, Alf Higginbotham, standing there in his grubby jeans with a sly, conspiratorial grin on his face. He had done some gardening for Gina once, till it had become clear he didn't know a weed from his left elbow.

"Had a good time, Mrs Paterwood?" Getting into the taxi, Gina stepped out of one of her best Louis Feraud courts. Her handbag fell and scattered once more and her skirt slipped. Velma roared with laughter and gave her a final push. And he drove past the car park just then. Colin Smallwood. On his way to do his round of patients on the expensive side of town, where the garages were all double or treble and the lawns were always shaved.

From her forward, half-prone position Gina saw him seeing her. Saw him take in Velma doubled up with raucous laughter. Saw him take in the onion-soup lover in his glistening suit with the unsuitable grey shoes. Saw him, above all, assess exactly the predicament she was in.

What with the curvature and the baldness of him, he made a sight with his mouth hung open. She swore he strained to see more in his inside car mirror as he drove on. It wasn't very gentlemanly of him.

She tried to pull her skirt zip up properly, beginning to feel cold all over and suddenly very, very sober.

Viciously she said to Velma, "You won't be seeing Onion Soup again, will you?"

"Course not."

There! Nailed! She would bring it up later. Velma's deliberate fib. Onion Soup had slipped Velma a piece of paper, no doubt with his phone number on it, just before he'd banged the taxi door shut on both of them.

No point in giving Alf Higginbotham fuel for his idle gossiping tongue. He was bolshie and sneering enough as it was. But she'd seen what transpired, all right, and it might be time to look up some other chums, even friends of Mummy's, and give Velma a rest.

You could go off people.

That was for sure. And on her birthday, Gina Paterwood wept.

2

Abercrombie's Aunt

"PEOPLE don't have aunts nowa-days," Lulu had said.

What is this advancing towards me in sensible ferry boats and freshly cleaned circus tent if it isn't an aunt? wondered Abercrombie. The same who had dispatched him south twenty years before, at age sixteen, braces through the loops in his Interlock underpants, four well smoothed pound notes in a monogrammed wallet, eight clean hankies, his Highers and a Biblical text under his clean copy of *How to Write* by Stephen Leacock.

"What have you got in here?" Her fibre suitcase was dislocatingly heavy and he staggered about the Euston concourse like a manic Max Wall. "Do you mean to tell me you still go in for those ironclad bloomers that used to festoon the kitchen pulley on wet Mondays?"

"I have a wee minding in there for you."

"What is it? The Stone of Scone?"

"No. Just home-baked sultana cake. I hope you're not going to talk about knickers in front of your intended," said Abercrombie's aunt, lemon-mouthed. "She'll wonder what sort of home you came out of. Where's this So Ho they're always talking about?"

"You wouldn't like it, Auntie."

"I might not like it, but I could always say I'd been there." Abercrombie's aunt steered a deliberate course towards the cafeteria. "Can we not have some tea and a bun or something? I want to discuss things with you before I meet your intended."

My intended what? Abercrombie wondered gloomily, as he queued with a tray, watching his aunt settle at a table like a carthorse backing into the shafts.

More like my *doomed*. He was perfectly happy with the relationship as it was and now the aunt would want to cross t's and dot i's. He and Lulu after long agonised discussions had decided that out of consideration for his aunt's Presbyterian principles, he would sleep on a camp bed in the living-room for the duration of her visit and Lulu would pretend the boxroom was her customary resting-place. He felt unreasonably irked to be denied the big bedroom where something unexpectedly good and joyful had been celebrated over the last seven months. But the aunt was the aunt. Jesus and No Quarter.

He would have to try to get her to understand that the relationship between himself and Lulu was an open one that she had no right to try to define or restrict. Looking over at her, he sighed at the near-impossibility of the task. Her recent letters had been heavy with intimations of mortality and prescience of Calls Home. Lulu might not know it, but she was due to be vetted as a vessel for the propagation of the Abercrombie species. Her Upper Second in History would be no protection. He felt a shrinkage in his loins and would not have been too surprised to look down and see red scabby knees above short trousers.

Provincial complexes that had troubled him not at all in recent years rose up to haunt the space behind the cafe tea urn. The need for Good Behaviour in front of the woman who had sacrificed all to bring him up; to revert to parochial Scot instead of cosmopolitan one. His aunt's burr-y Strathclyde patois had disengaged lever after lever so that his mind sped back to childhood trauma and insecurities.

He'd had someone on one of his recent programmes at the Beeb who'd gone into all that rather entertainingly. One of those young professors in a tweed tie and Red Baron flying jacket, discussing the dual nature of the Northern race, as he saw it torn between nostalgia for The Wee Hoose Amang The Heather and the need to dominate in the south.

Lulu had said with that sharp missionary look of hers that he should explore the dichotomy. He hadn't been all that sure what the word meant until recently, when he'd quietly looked it up, but now that its definition stared him in the face he realised Lulu had been right. Somehow he should have stonewalled the aunt.

Looking at her now, he felt as though his stomach were lined with the dry crumbs of digestive biscuits. Age had attacked that citadel of proletarian rectitude. Flesh was falling in soft, Plasticine folds from the massive, porridge-based frame, loose skin flapped in dewlaps about the formidable jaw. Seeing her raise an arm to wipe her forehead with a freshener pad, he remembered that hand parting and combing his hair with all the gentleness of a combine harvester. She had clicked lights out, refusing to let him read in bed. Made him walk on newspapers across the kitchen floor. Yet the light on her face when he read the lesson in church on his sixteenth birthday had been an awesome sight, winter sun on Ben Nevis. The bloody hat she wore now — surely it had made the trip south five years ago? She usually bought a new hat when she was going somewhere special. Was it too much of an effort these days? Guilt's hag-face nodded at him from behind the tea urn.

Abercrombie had sidled into television from journalism just in time, before the postwar Bulge, with their theses on Gramsci and Aspects of the African Novel, descended from the universities and took over. He had always looked better educated than he was. Reithian. "The perfect media man," Lulu teased. "All that breadth and no depth." "Send a fool to college," he retorted, "and all you get is an educated fool."

He slopped the tea into the tray, carrying the cups and a Chelsea bun of a particularly revolting yellow towards the aunt, knowing she would stare at it with the disbelief of someone from a region where cakes and tea-bread had been raised to an art-form. Having brought it, he would feel obliged to urge her not to eat it. He felt worn out already. He couldn't cope with two women. It was going to be worse, much worse than he predicted.

"Since you wouldn't bring her up to meet me, I've come down to see her," said the aunt now without preamble. "I want to see you settled, Archie. You're thirty-six. I know you say your career comes first, but you'll not be able to warm your feet on your work when you're fifty."

"Who warmed your feet?" he said, cornered.

"That was no fault of mine. A woman

has to wait to be asked."

"Not any more. Look, Auntie. About Lulu. She's very independent. She knows her way around. Researchers have to be tough, resourceful people."

"Don't apologise for her."

"For God's sake, I'm not doing that! I'm just saying: take her as you find her. Don't impose your ideas about marriage and such-like on her. She won't wear it."

He had seen that wait-and-see expression on his aunt's face before. Heaving her suitcase, he led the way in the search for a taxi, his expression woebegone and hopeless, that of a man who sees no way out.

"What's this?" demanded Abercrombie's aunt, several hours later. Rushing in from a heavy interview with a Saudi diplomat, Lulu had cooked one of her slapdash but exotic stews.

"Green pepper," said Lulu.

"Well, if you don't mind, dear, I'll not eat it." The aunt moved each offending green sliver to the side of her plate. "It might give me the wind. But the stew's very nice," she added, generously. "I can see Archibald has a good wee cook in you."

"I'm not his cook," said Lulu pleasantly. "Nor his bottle-washer, nor his anything else. We go shares."

"Oh, I know that," said the aunt innocently. "Archibald told me. You're an independent wee soul. They make the best kind of wives."

Abercrombie's eyebrows performed an explicit dance of warning across the table at Lulu. When the aunt had expertly and swiftly tidied up the kitchen and then retired to bed, Lulu exploded.

"I'm not letting this — this charade go on."

"Ignore her."

Lulu folded long be-jeaned legs under her and lit a Gauloise. "No," she said, decisively. "She's a woman, like me. A victim of role tyranny. Why shouldn't she go in for a spot of consciousness-raising like the rest of us?"

"Because she's getting on."

"So what? She's got all her marbles. Underneath all that repression and bigotry, there's a person waiting to be let out."

He kissed her absently, then protested,

"No. It's — it's a kind of violence, don't you see? Leave her be."

"Trust me."

"You're too clever by half. Too bloody consciousness-raised."

"You hate it because I had a university education and you didn't."

"I've told you before." His hand moved inside her blouse. "We don't get neurotic about education in the north. We're taught to spell and tie our shoe-laces then pointed towards the universe. Best thing."

As Abercrombie was putting out a programme the next day but Lulu was working on some notes at home, the two women were alone in the Shepherd's Bush flat. "I'll call you Jean," said Lulu, spearheading her attack. "You are not, after all, my auntie."

Abercrombie's aunt took in this declaration of intent in silence. She was busy polishing and tut-tutting over the scorch-marked dining-table and setting a trap with cheese for Lulu's tame mouse. The silence built up till Lulu made a pot of tea and, producing the home-made fruit cake, enthused over its flavour and moistness. The aunt's tight mouth relaxed in a careful simper.

"I don't normally like the English," she confessed. "But I think maybe you and me'll get on all right."

"Why don't you like them?" demanded Lulu.

"I once had an English neighbour that never washed her windows nor her curtains."

"You can't sink much lower than that."

"That's what I thought. You could hear her laughing and joking on a Sunday and men used to go into her house, with parcels."

"Parcels?"

"Chocolates and such. One even carried in a bunch of flowers."

"I sleep with him, you know. Archie."

The aunt's cup rattled down on its saucer and her mouth fell open, giving her a vulnerable, unprotected look that made Lulu feel, for a moment, the opposite of the parent who said yes, Virginia, there *is* a Santa Claus. Abercrombie's aunt rose and carried her crockery into the kitchen, making a big production out of washing up and putting away.

"Look, I'm sorry." Leaning against the lintel, Lulu looked it. "It's just that it — it feels so dishonest, not putting you in the picture. I'm fond of Archie but I've had other lovers, too. Ever since university."

If plaid skirts could look flurried, the aunt's did as she marched back into the sitting-room and flopped on the sofa.

"Do I shock you?"

Hands twisted a handkerchief. "I didn't come up the Clyde on a banana boat," the aunt protested. "I knew something was going on." They stared at each other. "Don't you *want* to get married? Don't you want to have children?"

"Not yet."

"Do you love Archie?"

"He's a nice man. A bit of an old woman, in some ways, I suppose because, if you don't mind me saying it, he was brought up by a spinster aunt. I mean sensitive — not effeminate. I like that. It counteracts my boldness. It works."

"I've never heard the like." The aunt looked pale, subdued. Lulu returned to her notes and when Abercrombie came in he looked from one to the other before prescribing large sherries all round.

"Not for me," said Abercrombie's aunt.

"Drink it up."

"It goes for my legs."

"Well, I need one." He looked beseechingly at Lulu. "One of the cameras packed up. There was a fight in the hospitality room. Sheeez! I'm glad to be home."

When Abercrombie looked at his aunt, her glass was empty and there was a flush on her cheeks.

"Give us some home news," he demanded.

With a smile of bravado she held the glass towards him. "That's quite a harmless wee drink. Give me a spot more and I'll see what I can think of. Oh, yes, I know. You remember Minnie Scoular, her that had the wee Jenny-a'-things shop on the corner? Well, it transpires that she'd been seeing a married man, every Wednesday when she goes into Glasgow, ostensibly to the wholesalers." She gave Lulu a look that might have been termed triumphant.

"And yon old Wattie Banks? The stories that have been going round about him! She wasn't his wife, you know, that one he had all the sons by. He knocked down a man for saying so, but a chiel came by from Carnwath and he had the right way of it."

"It sounds a scandalous place, where you come from," said Lulu softly.

"Well, you see, we have the television and all now. We keep up with the times."

"Auntie," said Abercrombie, concernedly. "You're all right, aren't you?"

"Of course she's all right," said Lulu. She leaned over and took the hand of Abercrombie's aunt, her gaze soft and even affectionate. "What was it like when you were growing up, Jean? Were your parents very strict? Did you go to dances? Did they make you work hard?"

"Hard?" Abercrombie's aunt put her other hand over Lulu's. "Do you know what I'm going to tell you?" Lulu shook her head. "They made me get up at five in the morning. It was still dark. I had to light the fire, clean the men's boots, make the porridge. I wasn't allowed to eat till everybody else had been seen to. If I protested, my father took the buckle end of his pit belt to me while my mother prayed in the corner. A life?" cried Abercrombie's aunt loudly. "You ask what kind of life I had. I had no sort of life at all. Work and kirk. Work and kirk. I was a slave. And when I was old enough I put half the country between us. I left them that had shown me no kindness. I got a place of my own and I worked at my dressmaking and I never went back."

"Did you know all this about Jean?" Lulu demanded.

Abercrombie shook his head. "She would never talk about the family. Would you? All I knew was that after my mother died — and my father who was a soldier in the war — you took me out of it and brought me up as your own."

"I gave you all I could," said the aunt. She stared at Abercrombie and then as though wound up began to talk about herself. She described her childhood, her early life in service, the clothes she had made for other people; judiciously, elaborating the bits that took her fancy, refusing to be drawn on other topics. But as suddenly as the flow of anecdote had begun, it ended.

"I'll away to my bed, Lulu," she said. "I'm tired." She put a hand on Abercrombie's face, consideringly, then bent and kissed him. "Goodnight, Archie son."

"I've never known her get on so well with anybody," said Abercrombie two days later. The aunt had been to the Tea Centre with Lulu and in Regent Street had picked a new hat. It was the first he'd ever seen her in without a brim and it suited her. "It's what you call a toque," his aunt enlightened him. She preened in front of the mirror.

"I like her," said Lulu, when Abercrombie's aunt had gone to bed. "Do you know what she's got away with her to read in there? In our lovely room which, pray God, we shall soon have back to ourselves? John Updike's *Couples*. Last night she was polishing off a Norman Mailer. What dark side of the Scots psyche is this I'm seeing?" she teased.

"She seems to be having a wonderful

time," said Abercrombie uncomprehendingly. "I would have taken a bet on it being a total disaster." He leaned over and kissed Lulu satisfactorily on the lips. "It's all down to you. You're a witch."

They both went to see Abercrombie's aunt off at the station. She wanted to cry, she said, but didn't want to spoil the effect of her new hat. "We'll see you soon," Lulu promised. "We'll be up in the summer."

As she walked back down the platform with Abercrombie, Lulu said, "Some day I might marry you, to please her. If you ask me."

"I'm thinking about it," he promised her. He looked embarrassed. "You gave her such a good time. Can I say it? I'm so — grateful."

"She needed taking out of herself. All that violence, all that repression."

"You got her to confide in you. You're a very clever woman."

Their arms entwined around each other's waists as they came out into the buffeting street wind. She was thinking of one particular confidence.

42

In the Tea Centre. When the aunt had said suddenly, "It's a different world we live in nowadays. In my days, if a woman had a bairn out of wedlock, she was branded a scarlet woman. Nowadays, all the thinking has changed." Her hand holding the teacup had trembled, ever so slightly as she'd appealed to Lulu. "Hasn't it?"

"Yes," Lulu had responded. "Nowadays, people are open." And after that they'd gone and bought that hat.

3

A Kindness

THEY bought the big rapacious house, with land, in Wales.

Plenty were doing the same. The hills were alive with the congratulatory sounds of those who had made a killing on the London property market. You met more film directors, telly producers, novelists, cartoonists, designers in these parts now than you might in Clapham or Notting Hill Gate. That's what they said. And she loved it. Was terrified in those early days that someone — Nemesis — would tap her on the shoulder and say it had all been a mistake, she would have to go back to the traffic jams, the fumes, the confusion of cultures, the dreadful push, shove and back-biting, the perpetual tension and wariness that was London.

She had rediscovered joy in a big untidy house that sat on a hill and gave

44

an endless view of the most meltingly wonderful natural beauty. Woods, water, farms, sheep, hills, dales, cattle. For the first time in her life she had dogs who could get their paws dirty, cats allowed the luxury of kittens and their children, hers and Tom's, had settled into their new life as though this was what they had been intended for, from the start. Maybe that was so. With Tom working hard at his word-processor at the top of the house — he worked on a variety of projects from biographies to articles about self-sufficiency and railways — she, a women's magazine journalist, wrote now when she felt like it. But mostly she worked at establishing them in the community, bringing her city skills to bear to make the parent-teachers' meetings more effective, to start up a dram club in the church hall a few miles away and to tackle problems like getting the post delivered on time or the roads sanded and verges cleared by the lackadisical local authority. She had a lot of energy and a mind trained to cope and organise.

And, of course, it was important to

cultivate their social life with their neighbours, who were rarer and more precious, being two, three, five, ten miles away. Mostly this was what they wanted, too, and she had established good relations with nearly everybody. Except old Gwilym at Nevvers Farm. He was one of the nearest and Rachel had decided it was one of her most interesting assignments, to break down his secretive, hill-farm taciturnity and have him telling her what it had been like when he first came here, with his now-dead wife, when the roads were barely existent and modern technology had not tamed so many of the problems for the country-lover. She even saw him cleaned-up and contributing, with his practical wisdom, to the Sunday lunch gatherings she had instituted once a month. But Jenny Hughes the Pub was more than cynical about her chances. "Black old heart, that one," she insisted. "Don't see you getting anywhere there, girl."

The Welsh were no different from anybody else, she told herself. In London she had had friends from practically every country you could think of, Arab friends,

West Indian friends, Aussie friends, American friends. Any suspicions that the Welsh were a little devious, a little watchful, that they waited and weighed you up and kept their appraisals of you to themselves, were nothing more than paranoia. Of course there was a fanatic fringe that didn't want anyone but the Welsh in Wales, but that kind of nationalism was as dead as Hitler, wasn't it? So it should be possible to make friends with old Gwilym, cheer him up a bit, widen his horizons. All that had happened was that he had got unused to company. Visits to the market town pubs when he had sheep to sell or fodder to buy were no substitute for real social intercourse. Rachel wanted him to know what it was like to have neighbours who cared about him. She said nothing to Tom but Gwilym was going to be her pet project. No man should be an island.

She took Thurlow, the black retriever, with her, the first time she walked past Nevvers Farm on her own, on a kind of speculative reccy.

It was little more than an extended cottage, roughly built of grey stone, with tiny windows and sills jammed with leggy geraniums. Rough wood and glass appendages had been built on at either side and at the back, besides the barns, were a number of mixed-medium erections, got together with brick, wood, corrugated iron and anything else to hand. There was a patch of kitchen garden and the beginnings of an orchard and even flowers that someone, possibly the late wife, had planted for cutting, but everything gave the impression of things started but given up before properly established or nurtured. Across from the house, in a field on the other side of the narrow track that eventually snaked over the mountain, there were hen-houses, bee skips and another rough barn housing hay. On the gate by the top of some broken steps there was a faded, hand-written board advertising fresh farm eggs and honey.

Rachel rang the bell at the side of the glass porch which sported yet more geraniums. It took some time, but eventually the shirt-sleeved, waistcoated, saturnine figure of her elderly neighbour appeared. She started to remind him they had been introduced at the market but he cut her short: "Aye, I know who y'are."

"I was wondering if I could have some eggs? Say a dozen. My hens haven't been laying."

"You're confident, aren't you?" he jeered. She did not know whether he was referring to her knowledge of the egg situation or whether it was an oblique criticism of her manner. Probably both.

"The notice says — "

"Aye. Notices can say what they like. I'll see what I can do."

He disappeared back into the depths of the house and returned with two cardboard egg boxes, patting down the lids. "Just new-laid, these. Fresh today."

"How much?"

He named a sum that seemed to her a bit excessive, but they were new-laid so she paid up without demur.

"Like it here?" he demanded, still in the same jeering tone.

Rachel swept an arm towards the hills, bathed in afternoon sunshine, sheep-speckled and tranquil.

"How could I not? It's so wonderful

to live where you can taste the air. If you know what I mean. I can't get over the contact with living things. With animals. We'd all forgotten what nature was about." She smiled engagingly.

"Wait till the snow comes."

"It'll be fun." Her face shone with the expectation of a winter and Christmas out of the picture books. Sledging and bringing home the logs and hot noggins in the little pub in the hollow by the church.

"You'll sink in up to your armpits. The beasts'll die on you."

She thought he said it with a certain unnecessary savour, but tactfully changed the subject.

"I was wondering if you'd like to come and have lunch with us this coming Sunday? We're having a few neighbours in."

He pretended not to hear her. "Six foot deep, the snow gets," he said. "And that's a mild winter. When it's bad the power goes, the telly, the lot."

"We don't depend on the telly, Gwilym." There, she had established first-name terms. She was pleased with

50

herself for not taking offence at his rebuffing ways.

"I do. I like all them quiz games and the cop films and murder. I like them murder films," he said firmly.

She could hardly make deprecating noises at this, as she might have done with the children. She had to accord him his full rights as a grown-up, democratic citizen and that included watching quiz shows and murder films, if that was what he liked. He was watching her face very closely, almost greedily, with his small, lively, anarchic, mean black eyes set in the grubby, lined, leathery face. She knew she might not be in the presence of a cultivated intelligence, but it was a cutting, active one, fully aware of the games people played.

She swung the conversation towards him.

"You must get lonely," she said sympathetically, "living up here by yourself."

He said, in his jeering tone she was finding increasingly difficult to take, "*You* might. It might get lonely for you. I was bred here. I've lived here all my days. I *belong* here. So loneliness don't come into it."

He did not come on the Sunday, although she had made provision for him. Katherine Wilk, another ex-Londoner who ran a bed-and-breakfast and craft workshop, said "He'll be too busy selling off his ancient curdled eggs to Sunday drivers."

"What do you mean?" asked Rachel, colouring.

"God knows how long they lie around. He's even been known to pass off shop-bought ones when his hens are off laying," said Jenny Hughes the Pub.

"Oh," said Rachel faintly. So she had been right. The omelette she'd made for breakfast this morning had been a bit niffy. She felt squeamish. How could he, the little toad? But she'd continue to be nice to him, to be neighbourly, to be friendly. Rachel did not give up easily and being friendly with Gwilym was part of her masterplan for settling in the hills. Was even, if you like, propitiation for coming in like the Goths with rude metropolitan ways, for replacing lore and legend with hi-tech and know-how. But if this wave of newcomers like herself was not about communications, in every way, what was it about?

No use learning to use Fax and word-processors, all the paraphernalia of instant contact, no point in having hand telephones, being able to use all the wondrous adjuncts of the information technology, if you could not communicate with the other inhabitants of your new Eden. And that meant even Gwilym.

"Leave the old bugger be," said Tom, not overly keen on his neighbour since that August day when they'd lost some of their first livestock, healthy young sheep — gone out one morning to find them lying on their backs with their feet turned up, a cataclysmic sight, as Rachel had named every one, in the old Biblical manner of the Scottish crofters she'd read about somewhere.

"Could 'a told you that," Gwilym had said, when he'd encountered him while out looking for the vet. "They eat all that lush grass and their stomachs swell up and the first frosts get them."

"You could have warned me," Tom had muttered under his breath and he had sworn Gwilym's minimal mean line of a mouth had actually smiled as he'd answered, "You never asked me."

Rachel took Harry and Annabel with her on her next visit to Gwilym's farm. They were nice, disarming children — at least she thought so — and Annabel had a school project about bees and honey, so Rachel hoped Gwilym might show them the hives. They went bearing gifts as part of the softening-up process — woollen mitts Annabel had knitted at school and a scarf with several dropped stitches which Rachel was nonetheless proud of having finished.

"I thought," she said, handing them over to the farmer on his doorstep, "that they might come in handy of a cold morning. When you're gathering the eggs and such-like." Their eyes met and she wondered if he felt guilty over the disgraceful business of the rotten eggs. He took the gifts gracelessly, without a word of thanks.

He refused to let them look at the hives saying it might frighten the bees. "Noisy kids are bad for them, he told Rachel defiantly, although Harry and Annabel had stood beside her silent and wide-eyed while their mother went through the ritual of propitiation.

When they walked away, Harry said angrily, "Did you see his dog? It cowered. I think he kicks it. I think he's a horrible old man."

"I think he's cruel to animals," Annabel agreed tearfully. "And they are poor dumb things, Mum. The beasts of the field and we have dominion over them. It means we should take care of them properly. It's what we were told by Miss Marchbanks."

"I don't think he's cruel," said Rachel, thoughtfully. "Not actually cruel. He's probably tougher than we are. His dog has to know he's master because it's a sheepdog and has to take orders from him." But she had seen the scruffy dullness of the dog's coat and wondered if the kids were right.

When she recounted the latest incident to Katherine Wilk, her friend advised her to give up on the old farmer. "He's forgotten how to relate properly to other folk," said Katherine. "That's if he ever knew." But there was a stubborn Pollyanna streak that had always been there with Rachel. She had served midnight soup to drop-outs near Waterloo and Christmas dinner to tramps at Nine Elms. She had not given up on trying to improve the world and the Gwilyms in it. Else what was a heaven for?

* * *

The autumn was glorious. Nature the painter took out the whole box of colours and trees, skies, fields blended into a panorama as clear as a china plate and subtle as a Monet palette. Rachel left Tom at work and strode out over the hills, stopping where the water ran to see it sparkle on rocks, marvelling at heather and lichen, listening to the muted sounds of birds and livestock.

Sometimes wild ponies froze like a film track or big black clouds pregnant with rain sent her scuttling to a friend's house for a snatched mug of coffee and a gossip. Katherine said she was a right Emily Brontë and she did not mind that. She felt that living in cities had somehow come near to smothering her soul, that she could not get enough of restorative freedom, that somehow a kind of birthright had been handed back to her.

Nor was winter, the first real winter, as tough as Gwilym had prophesied. The snow, when it came, did not lie for too long and was exaggeratedly picturesque without lying too deep. Certainly the winds were cold and the frost bit hard, but they congratulated themselves on not having more livestock than they could cope with and the animals themselves soon indicated their own needs.

The social life was all the jollier for being unforced. There were some formidable cooks among the wives, especially the indigenous Welsh ones, and delicious soups, marvellous ragouts, splendid cakes and puddings welcomed you in out of the cold after an exhilarating, sometimes alarming, drive over icy tracks, and hot punches, wine, whisky, flowed hospitably. People *cared*, Rachel told Tom, really cared for each other. Friendships were much closer because there were fewer of you and fences were rapidly mended after any fall-out because you could not afford to lose a helping hand, a source of good advice. That's what the hills were teaching them, said Rachel. The truth of the old adage, that we must love one another, or die. Wasn't that Auden, Tom asked, or Eliot? It's the apothegm that matters, Rachel replied. She was very happy in her Eden. Unreasonably so, she thought afterwards. The move had been mostly her idea, and she had thought of it as some almost supernatural benison. It could so easily have gone horribly wrong.

The affair that started between Tom and Katherine Wilk, about a year after Rachel and Tom had moved to the big rapacious house on the hill, was never a blatant one. Was even understandable, given that Tom was going through a difficult time professionally and had reached that retrospective point that everyone does after a major upheaval, where you start to remember the good things about where you once lived. He had liked keeping up the odd contact in the Fleet Street pubs, nipping out to

Docklands to chew the fat with the odd features editor. The disillusion he'd felt with his publisher before the move had softened into fond, hazy recollections of outrageous good times at book lairs and signing sessions. He even missed the bitching. Brief forays back to London left him disorientated and fed up, but he had hidden all this from Rachel, or most of it, because she was so blissfully secure and happy and they both had such a big emotional commitment. Katherine Wilk's chivvying, raucous good humour and readiness to read his need for some outside source to confide in had been all too providential.

Rachel saw them laughing together at parties, of course she did. She was glad Tom had made a friend. He needed someone to lift him out of his introspection at times and she had never thought you should stop going out towards other people just because you were married. They had a solid marriage and she trusted Tom. If she thought Katherine's husband Arthur looked a shade miserable and withdrawn, that seemed to be the norm for him. After a few drinks he usually cheered up and could be heard telling quite rude but funny jokes putting down the English.

No one dropped hints. Rachel was more into animal husbandry and was often tired, pleasantly so, when they went out, her lungs washed with the fresh, winey air, her muscles relaxed after labour. Perhaps she had let the sharp, observant side of her nature, the one that had made her a good journalist, lapse into unseeing. At any rate, the affair was at its full-blown, unrenunciatory zenith when she got the first wind of it from Gwilym.

She was still keeping an eye on him. Dropping in with periodicals, the odd pot of jam or chutney. And still getting what Tom had inelegantly called the bum's rush. She was, she argued, prepared to take the old man for what he was.

"Don't you trust that one that does the bed and breakfast." He kept her at the doorstep, his grasping old hand quick to take the blackcurrant preserve from hers, his gaze directed, maddeningly, down the dust-track, anywhere but meeting hers.

"You know I don't gossip about

friends, Gwilym."

"She's no friend. Craft-shop suits her. Crafty craft-shop." He was fond of gnomic utterances.

"What are you saying, Gwilym?" she asked calmly.

"I never said nothing," he said blandly. For once he met her eye. She could have sworn there was something almost human in the way he looked at her. Not fond. But human. It disturbed her far more profoundly than anything he had said. She walked away from him, for once not rhapsodising mentally about the exquisite beauty of the scene from his particular knoll, for once without a word for his old donkey who rolled up to call her. After that, she noticed everything, saw every stolen smile awarded to Tom by Katherine, every gaze that locked, every brush of hands, every brown study her husband lapsed into after he'd been out on his own.

And, of course, the time came when she threw the accusation of unfaithfulness at him and he responded, not by denial, as some desperate part of her had still hoped, but by admission. It was a very bitter thing for Rachel to hear the man she had loved devotedly and exclusively for fifteen years declare his love for someone else.

After that part of it was over — the shouting, the tears, the awful recriminations, the things neither of them wanted to hear, the silences, the desolation — Rachel reached the point where she was able to offer Tom his freedom. Some similar kind of accommodation was reached by Katherine and her partner, but instead of coming to Tom, Katherine headed back for London.

"Go on," urged Rachel bitterly. "Follow her. You know it's what you want. You never wanted to live in the country anyway."

"I don't want to go back there," said Tom, realising it was true and realising also, with the poet, that things like a wife and children could melt the very heart of stones. Especially children. Once he had decided he would try and make a go of it again with his family, it seemed to him his life entered an altogether deeper and more meaningful phase. The strange thing was that when Katherine Wilk was no longer there, he could scarcely even recall what her face looked like. Perhaps he saw himself now as a little bit of a boyo: whatever his self-image, he was able to live with it.

Rachel knew the roads to saving a marriage very well. From the depths of her inexperience she had advised countless friends over the years when they had run into difficulties. The best thing to do when emotions got out of hand was to seek professional help and counselling. This she and Tom did and after a while she acknowledged she could go on with the marriage. She did not feel very differently but the charade had somehow salved her pride and at least she knew herself better now than she had ever done before.

The consensus at the Post Office and General Store was that afterwards Rachel did not have the same enthusiasm for local affairs. She did not go near Nevvers Farm now and Gwilym's donkey called to her in vain for a piece of apple. Why should she take tomato chutney to someone who had been only too ready to point out that great, gaping hole in her emotional life, the time her husband had let his eye wander? No doubt Gwilym had thought he was doing her a service.

"How are you there?" he would call to her but she always walked past him with her head averted, as though she saw something riveting elsewhere and always her heart thundered and the tears sprang to her eyes and once again she was wrung by something bitterer than grief and more lasting than forgiveness.

4

Rose Would Be A
Lovely Name For It

ANNETTE BASSIE, sixteen, of
112 Cumberland Place, Chennock,
an overspill estate of the outer
London suburbs, walked carefully along
the grass verge on her six-inch cork
wedgies, avoiding the dog excrement and
thinking of little babies in yellow stretch
jumpsuits with Snoopy on them.

She saw this particular baby, hers,
being held up by Damon, who would
be wearing a denim two-piece and an
Afro hairdo and shiny white clumpy
wedgies which Annette really fancied at
the moment. There would be a struggle,
getting Damon to buy the wedgies, but
she had nearly eight months to work
on him to get him used to the idea.
Anyway . . . Damon would be holding
up the baby, who would be laughing
and dimpling like in the adverts for

baby powder and she would be standing nearby with a proud smile and maybe a yellow dress with those sort of cap sleeves. Hair up or down? She couldn't quite decide but up would maybe look more in keeping with having a baby.

A him, would it be, then? She didn't mind if it was a her because Jackie Prince's little Theresa Jayne was ever so sweet, with little soft padded hands and long lashes and curly hair and you could dress little girls up ever so nice . . .

There, she'd done it. Stepped in dog's woopsie because she hadn't been thinking of where she was going. She sat down on the grass verge, removing the shoe and cleaning it on the grass, aggrieved out of all proportion to the incident and the tears running down her face so fast she couldn't stop them. She put up the back of her hand and all that bloody mascara that they'd said was waterproof came away on her skin.

"I'm afraid so, Annette," Dr Ramsay had said, shaking his head at her. "Didn't they teach you about contraception at school?" She had been too weary to explain to him what Damon had said about it being all right if he took his thing away in time, and, anyway, they hadn't done it all that often and it hadn't made sense to take the Pill every day when she and Damon might go quite a long time without him taking her up the fields or her Mum being out and nothing good on the telly.

He had quite a kind face, Dr Ramsay, but his trousers smelled and there was a brown line along his lower lip from smoking. She'd nearly said, "What business is it of yours?" but she'd been feeling too dizzy. He'd started asking about whether she'd told her mother and sending up a social worker and she'd begun to cry because the social worker would be Mrs Berry and her mother thought Mrs Berry was a cow and had told her so to her face.

"We'll sort something out," Dr Ramsay had said, vaguely, patting her on the back. "And then you get yourself down to that birth-control clinic and take proper precautions. You hear me?"

She'd nodded, and come out, and it hadn't been bad, walking along the grass in the middle of the morning, seeing mums putting sausages and Surf and Mother's Pride loaves and tins of peas and frozen crinkle-cut chips and Six Selected Iced Fancies into those wire baskets under the prams and little kids with green iced lollies dribbling down their fronts running in and out of the shops and touching the mongrel dogs tied to pram handles.

"Do you take this woman . . . ?" She stopped crying as the picture popped up in her mind of her and Damon getting married. She was all enveloped in white, all over, like in fine Terylene net curtains only it was her wedding veil, from whence her face peeped out, rosy and beautiful as the dawn. The girl of his dreams. Memories are made of this. Make it a wedding to remember. Only Damon stayed thin and angular and even in the picture she couldn't get him out of those lowslung denims, so tight at the crotch it was a wonder, her mum said, it didn't ruin his prospects, and that white tee shirt with Billy Bremner on it because his dad came from Leeds.

She got up, a little groggily, knowing it wasn't going to be like that. If she went down the supermarket, Damon might be bringing in the wire trollies or unloading the van and she could get speaking to him. She didn't like seeing him in the long white overall. It made him look too small and young. But she felt very desperate. "In view of your case history," Dr Ramsay had said, "we might be able to arrange for you to abort this child. Good gracious, lassie, you are no' much more than a child yourself."

She looked inside the supermarket and just past a display of chocolate digestive biscuits on unrepeatable offer she saw Damon putting bottles of malt vinegar on the shelves. She grabbed a wire basket and walked up to him.

"Congratulations," she said. "You are going to become a dad."

His face was a study. It went as white as his overall.

"Not here," he hissed.

"Gotta be here," she said, relentlessly. "I'm supposed to be having an operation to get rid of it."

"Oh, Jesus," said Damon. He dropped a quart bottle of malt vinegar and it hit the supermarket floor with a resounding thwack, breaking and sending the brown liquid over an unbelievably large area of floor.

"Bloody go," he said to Annette, as the supervisor bore down on the scene with tch-tch written all over her body. Annette backed away from the vinegary tide. She went outside and peered over a placard offering marmalade at drastic reduction. She saw Damon laboriously wipe up and then fetch a mop and bucket to wash the floor. It was going to take too long, he would never be finished, so she walked away. She had had no breakfast that morning and she felt suddenly and ravenously hungry; she could eat beefburgers and chips and beans but when she got home it had to be toast. She ate two slices and drank two mugs of milky tea with a lot of sugar in it. She looked at the paper from Sunday and a girl with no clothes on: "Aeron is going places. A part in a new werewolf film and that of a sexy waitress in the TV series 'Dr Banks, Superstar', are rewards for this uplifting view of her very vital statistics."

The front door banged and Mrs Bassie

returned from her morning cleaning job. The woman she worked for, who had three teenage daughters, had given her some worn clothes which she bore in on a note of minor triumph in two bulging paper carriers.

"Get us a cup of tea, Annette," she begged. She threw off her coat, saying, "I'm buggered, so I am."

"You been down the Labour?" Mrs Bassie demanded, gulping down the tea Annette put before her.

"Yeh," Annette lied.

"Nothing doing?"

"No, nothing doing." Feeling the need to convince, Annette added, "There was a job at the baker's but I said I couldn't do it for my eczema."

Her mother looked at her suspiciously, then began pulling out the cast-off clothing. Annette fingered it mutinously. The girls who had worn these went to a fee-paying school and sat O levels. Her mother sometimes mimicked the way they said, 'Hellow' to her, patronisingly, as she tidied up their rooms. They had a sauna in the garden and went to France for their holidays. She hated the feeling of gentility that came from their clothes. "I'm not wearing any of that rubbish," she told her mother.

Mrs Bassie tried on a short-sleeved jumper in apple green that stretched perilously across her generous bosom.

"This is all right," she approved. Annette looked at her detachedly. She was all wrong, her mother, the way she looked. Those big boobs, the long, knobbly-kneed legs in the youthful wedgies, the peroxide hair, were meant for a younger face. Her mother's face was wrinkled, anxious, lived-in, middle-aged. She wished she didn't have to tell her mother about the baby, what with her older brother being in the open prison for a fire he had never done and little Tone stealing and going through this phase of not wanting to go to school and Dad having fallen off the ladder and being dead quite a long while.

"Mum," said Annette, fearfully.

"Just a minute," said Mrs Bassie. She rose and switched on the television at full volume. Then she brought out an elderly Hoover and switched it on also, placing it as near the inside television walls as possible.

"I met that black cow down the bus-stop," Mrs Bassie shouted. "I told her I'd been down the Council about that bloody industrial sewing-machine and she turned round and said she never had one. It went till half-past two this morning *and* he had his bongoes out. I never slept a wink."

"But she's out next door," Annette protested.

"He isn't," said Mrs Bassie. "He don't put his nose out till it's time to go down the betting-shop." She grew tired of the self-created din and switched off both machines. "It's like living in the middle of the bloody jungle," she complained. "And on Sunday she'll be down the mission hall in that lemon tulle hat crying out that Jesus saves. He won't save her if I get hold of her by that coconut matting she calls hair."

"Mum," said Annette, "I'm going to have a little baby."

"Decent people," said Mrs Bassie, continuing her harangue, "decent people don't have a chance."

"Mum," repeated Annette, "I said, I've been down the doctor and I'm going to have a little baby."

Mrs Bassie sat down suddenly, gripping the edge of the Formica-topped table.

"Eh?" she said.

"They're sending Mrs Berry down and I might have to have an abortion. Because of my case history."

"Oh God," said Mrs Bassie, gulping for air. "Didn't they learn you nothing about that at school?"

"I was off with rheumatic fever," said Annette. "I only picked up bits from the other girls."

"I thought you knew," said Mrs Bassie, bewilderedly.

"Knew what, Mum?"

"How to stop it."

"Don't cry, Mum." Mrs Bassie was weeping, as someone used to it, soundlessly and efficiently, putting big, rough hands up to dash away the tears. "I could have it," said Annette. "Me and Damon could get married and get a council house and have it."

"He's a bloody little runt," said Mrs Bassie, a shade more hopefully. "What

74

age is he? Fifteen? Sixteen?"

"He's sixteen next week," said Annette. "I mean, he's working, he gets eighteen quid a week."

"You'll never get a place," said Mrs Bassie.

"Could we live here?"

"It wouldn't be allowed. We'd be overcrowded."

"I could sleep with you and Damon with Tone. For a bit." Her mother shook her head, but a little more kindly.

"You randy little bitch," she said, almost fondly. "What you want? Boy or girl?"

"I think girl, really," said Annette, smiling for the first time that day. Her hair, dyed blonde like her mother's, peaked out in front of her pale face, like a cap. She put skinny arms over her flat little bosom.

"You can dress 'em up nice," said Mrs Bassie.

"I thought Rose would be a nice name for it," said Annette, boldly. "Rose Yvonne."

"You thought if it's a boy?" demanded her mother, sharply.

"Dean or Larry."

Mrs Bassie considered these and did not dismiss them out of hand. "We could get your cousin Marilyn's pram and cot," she said, "and you get second-hand things down the clinic that are ever so new-looking."

Annette decided she would not remind her mother what Dr Ramsay had said about getting an abortion. She had already decided to go ahead and have the baby. It hadn't been something she had thought out, carefully, the way she thought out what she would wear to a dance, for example. It was just a foregone conclusion. She could see the baby as plain as she could see the nose on her mother's face. Rose Yvonne or Dean. In a big cream pram. With a wire basket underneath and a dog tied to the handle.

She snivelled a little, worrying about Mrs Berry coming up to see her mum. She said, "I thought of getting it a yellow jumpsuit, with that Snoopy dog on it. Jackie had one for her Theresa Jayne, only it was an apple on it."

"An apple?"

"Instead of Snoopy."

"Yellow does for boy or girl."

"Yeh. That's what I thought."

★ ★ ★

"She can't be allowed to have it," said Dr Ramsay.

"He must have a leaky bladder," thought Caroline Berry. Some doctors, the kind who liked their patients, got ropey-looking as they got older. But he had a reputation for good diagnosing, this one, and the solid matrons going through the Change sat out the long minutes in his surgery for the chance of a reassuring word with him, just as the nervy young ones took the Valium prescriptions from his hand with the faith of votaries taking the Sacramental wafer. Last of a dying breed, he was. A doctor who gave himself. He gave her a piercing, aware look and said crisply, "Well?"

"You tell me, doctor."

"She could probably scrape through on the physical side, with great care, perhaps in hospital. But she's a hysterical child, she's been in care, her mother's been through too much. The skids are under the whole family."

"Right."

"You'll take care of it?"

"Yes."

"Up to three months, it's only tissue, isn't it?" Caroline thought. Have we a right to bring babies into the world who will be neglected, perhaps battered, who will have the Big Hand against them right from the start? No, we haven't, she thought, but a persistent other voice was putting up other arguments, saying stridently, who was she to decide? Was life, no matter how tragic or brutal, not a precious gift they had no right to withhold? As if there are any easy answers, thought Caroline, wearily. I wish I didn't have to keep facing them. I wish I didn't have to take responsibility. Mrs Bassie will insult me again. I wish I didn't have to see her. I'll see anybody but her. Dr Ramsay's cool, dedicated face came back to her. She'd promised him she'd take care of it. She wouldn't have any lunch. Just a cup of coffee, and then she'd go.

Annette went down the big block at

the end of the estate where Damon lived and waited for him by the brick wall that among other graffiti had a slogan saying 'Send the Pope to the Moon'. At six-thirty he emerged from the flat entrance and she could see at once there had been trouble. One eye was a puffy red and he had been crying.

"Was it your dad?" she asked.

"He bloody thumped me," said Damon, beginning to weep again. "Said I could get out and never come back. I ain't going back there, never."

"Oh, Gawd," said Annette. "And I was hoping your mum would give us a room."

"She never said a bleeding thing," said Damon. "Just sat there."

"What we gonna do?"

"Go up to your mum's."

Annette said, red-faced, "I don't want to go up there just yet. She's had the social worker in there today. She'll want me to have the operation now, if I know anything."

"Maybe you should."

"Don't want to."

"Where can we go?" he demanded, desperately.

"Anywhere," she said, blankly. She began to move away as though in a dream.

He was still overwrought. Across the street stood a clapped-out old banger of a car, rust enveloping its radiator and bumpers.

"We'll take our Syd's car," Damon decided. "He can't drive it till he gets his licence back."

"Will it go?" asked Annette doubtfully. She got in. After a few doubtful wheezes, the car moved forward. Damon drove it carefully round the estate then along a quiet road leading to countryside.

"You'll get in ever such trouble," said Annette, but she was quite enjoying it. Damon had his tongue out and was concentrating on his steering. He had been up before the court for taking cars before, but what they didn't understand was that he just *knew* how to drive them, it was second nature to him. They drove past a golf club and then they went driving past small farms and riding stables and small holdings. It was a sunny evening, cool, fresh and invigorating.

"It's like an adventure," said Annette. Damon looked ever so small, like a little boy driving the dodgems at the fair. Grave doubts arose in her mind about the possibility of getting him into a denim two-piece or of him sanctioning an Afro hair-style or looking remotely father-like. She gave a troubled sigh.

"I know a place," said Damon suddenly, "where we could go and they wouldn't find us."

"Where?"

"It's just up here. You go along this sort of road that's been made by lorry wheels and there's a sort of wood. Nobody would see us. We could make a fire."

He looked at her and her spirits rose at his intense, excited expression. He was going to take care of her. It was possible he really loved her. The car would be like a little house. All their own. Maybe they would never have to go back and she would never have to know the outcome of the discussion, if that was the word, between her mother and Mrs Berry.

Damon swung the car up the rutted track and into the edge of the lightly wooded area. All around were fields and there was only one sign of habitation, a white farmhouse with broken-down outbuildings, lying several fields away.

"I could go down there, after dark," said Damon, "and pick us up something to eat."

"How do you mean?"

"Potatoes, fruit. Might even be able to get into the house and get milk and bread and stuff."

She drew up her shoulders in scandalised delight. "They might get you, Damon."

"Nah." He smiled at her, the bruise from his father's fist coming up blue and purple under his eye. She put out her hand and touched it. "Is it bad?"

"Nah." He caught her hand and they held each other close. It was all right for them to make love because the baby had happened anyway and couldn't happen again.

Annette had some fruit pastilles in her jacket pocket and they smoked the last four of Damon's cigarettes. The evening deepened in gradual layers of blue until it was quite dark, but there was a moon and shapes remained clear and unalarming.

They moved into the back seat of the car where it was warmer and huddled together, talking and planning.

Some of the things Damon planned, like going to Ireland or America, Annette knew to be impractical. What would they do for money?

"We can sleep in the car," she argued. "It can be our house like. Even when the baby comes. And during the day we can go out and work and get some money."

"I can't drive it about no more," said Damon. "I ain't got a licence, you know."

"But if we stayed here."

"How'd we get to work?"

"Maybe there's a country bus."

He acknowledged this possibility. After that they gave up planning because their brains were getting tired. Annette persuaded Damon against going to the farm and instead they exchanged reminiscences of their childhood.

"What was the very best Christmas you could ever remember?" she demanded.

"In the home," Damon answered. He had told her about it before, but she liked to hear and he liked to talk about it. "Time me mum left me dad and he went into hospital with his nerves. We had turkey and plum pudding and trifle twice over. And in the morning after breakfast, we all went to church."

"I had new clothes from the skin out. Shoes and everything. We never had no cast-off clothes there. The house-mother took us into the shop and we got everything new. And then after dinner with paper hats and those things you blow and they curl out we had a rest and then the superintendent dressed up as Father Christmas and gave each child a toy. They were good toys, too, nothing rubbishy. I got a football game 'cos it was what I asked for. They tried to give you what you asked for. I could hardly believe it. It was great."

"Yeh," Annette gave a dreamy sigh. "I think I would have liked being in a home for Christmas."

"Nah," he said, smiling at her affectionately. "You wouldn't have liked all them baths and things. And they wasn't like your own mum and dad, know what I mean?"

They was nice, and they taught you to talk proper but you couldn't tell them to sod off, like you could your old man.

"They never hit you, did they?" asked Annette. "My turn now, Damon, to tell you about my best Christmas. It was when I got a proper ballet frock for dancing in, in the school concert. Miss Bains was going to make me one at the school but me mum got this lovely flare-free net in a beautiful pink colour and she went up Mrs Andrews, the dressmaker, and got her to make it proper.

"And when I got up Christmas morning, it was lying at the bottom of my bed, and there was a pair of them silver dancing-slippers in my size."

She held him very tight, as though he was this marvellous memory, and shivering with recollected pleasure she said, "Me and the boys all clubbed together and we went down Woolworth's after Christmas and we bought my mum a locket to go round her neck saying 'To the best mum in the world'. She liked it ever so much. It'll be nice when it's Christmas with the baby, Dame. We can get a little tree and put a star on it and cut out things from milk-bottle tops.

"A real tree," he said.

"Yeh, they're best. Not one of them silver, made ones."

"I'm frightened about you having the baby. Maybe they won't let you."

"Don't be frightened," she said, with a tremendous feeling of tenderness welling up inside her, so that she could not resist pulling his head down to her bosom and cradling it, almost as though he were the baby. "It'll be all right. I love you, Damon. This car is our little house and we are safe here. They can't get at me here."

The moon sailed behind a cloud and the landscape became mysterious, undefined. Damon's breathing became regular and with his head on her shoulder he went into a deep, dreamless sleep. Annette pushed her face into his hair, liking his human animal smell. Soon she, too, was sleeping, curled into a foetus-like ball on the back seat of the rusty car.

★ ★ ★

86

"Their lives are two-dimensional, cardboard cutouts, said Caroline Berry to her husband, Simon, pouring him more warm red wine. "They have no cultural heritage now, just the telly. They *had* something when they lived in the East End, even if it was just 'Knees Up Mother Brown' in the pub on a Saturday night or hop-picking every year in Kent. Now they're just overspill — annoying rubbish to be packed into concrete boxes. All the individuality's been knocked out of them. Bloody bureaucracy has knocked them sideways."

Simon sighed. He gave the impression of only half listening. He *was* only half listening. Caroline felt that these days he was getting farther and farther away from contact, like a swimmer setting out across the ocean. O Simon, don't leave me. She didn't know how to make him turn back.

She kept on talking. She had had a terrible interview with Mrs Bassie, who had thrown a half-empty Coke tin at her, and then Annette had disappeared altogether and Dr Ramsay had accused her, unjustly, of being clumsy.

"Come to bed," said Simon, peremptorily, after the meal. Their bed-sitter was large, airy, with a nice Habitat bedspread Caroline liked and Soutine and Bonnard prints they'd brought back from the Museum of Modern Art in Paris.

Simon's desk, piled with his philosophy books and novels in the original French and German, stood by the window and the branches of a sycamore tree waved through the glass in friendly fashion. When he got his PhD he would be happier, released, not beholden, galvanised. It couldn't be easy for him just now. Caroline stroked his hair with a delicate touch.

He caught her wrist.

"How do you know," he demanded, "that up there their lives aren't fuller, happier than ours?"

"They haven't read Thomas Mann," she teased.

"They've never heard of Wittgenstein."

"They think Mahler's that wrestler with the hood over his head and slits for the eyes."

"And that Hockney's some kind of cheap wine."

They laughed and he held her close and began to make complicated love to her, kissing her here and there, till she panted a little and said, "Now, darling, now." But he lay back, flicking his wrists back on the pillow, groaning and saying, "It's no bloody good, I can't."

"It'll be all right," she soothed.

"No, Caro. We both know it won't." He got up abruptly, zipping on his jeans, lighting a Gauloise, striding up and down the room, slim-hipped and agitated.

"Simon. Please! Please let's talk about it."

He turned an angry, tortured mask of a face towards her.

"I don't want to talk! Something's wrong —

"You don't love me any more."

"And all you can say is let's talk about it."

He sat down beside her. "Caro, are you aware how much you talk? How sensible, how pragmatic you are! It's like making love to your old headmistress in the junior school."

She gave a cry of pain and he said contritely, "No, I don't mean that — "

89

"You aren't attracted to me! Why don't you say it?"

"Because it's not true. But — " He paused.

"No. Go on. You must say it."

"I don't want to upset you."

"Please," she insisted, stonily.

"Well. Do you ever feel that what we have is — is a sterile thing? We've put these restraints, the restraints of marriage, on ourselves, and marriage turns out to be a tense, watching relationship in a single room. No babies. You taking the Pill and getting bloated — "

"And keeping you." Her venom was deadly.

"Yes," he admitted. "Keeping me. A process of rational emasculation." He rose. "I'm getting out, Caro. Let's call it a day."

She rose and buttoned up her dress. She could feel her nipples, still hard and engorged from caresses and her vagina, wet and slippery. A terrible primal need to throw herself on his mercy, to plead that he should take her, give her a child, fill her womb, overcame her, and with it, as always, the weary realisation that there were too many children in the world, not enough rooms to hold them. Too many careless Bassies, that the Simons and Carolines had to make up for.

But at that moment, she would not have cared. She wanted him to come to her and the situation was that they could no longer make it together: that they had held back once too often. World was not rational. World was mouth and breast and womb and penis: world was skin and hair and semen. And world was the starving children of Ethiopia, who every night paraded before her mind's eye when she said her formless prayers: big-bellied, hollow-eyed, inhabitants of the hell made by those who would not take the Pill, adopt the coil, remember the sheath. Who would not think. Who had not been to university or entered the world of books and words and theories and principles.

Simon came out from the kitchenette where he had put the kettle on.

"I'll make the coffee," he said, in his normal voice.

"You *can* go, you know," she said, tonelessly.

He went over to her. Held her briefly, by the arms.

"It's temporary, of course," he said, shrugging. "But it worries a man."

"I know."

"Be patient."

"Of course."

"I'm sorry."

"So am I."

★ ★ ★

"What made you think you'd get away with it?"

Mrs Bassie took a long swig of tea, lit a cigarette and took a deep inhalation of smoke. She looked at Annette with genuine curiosity.

"We was going to stay there," cried Annette, defiantly. "We was going to stay there and sleep in the car."

"Don't be so bloody daft."

"I know couples what have done that. I've read it in the papers. When they couldn't get a house."

"Then they had no more bloody sense than you have. Daft gits! You must have known Damon's dad would go down

92

the cop-shop. You must have known Syd wouldn't stand for having his car took."

"Rotten old car," said Annette, sulkily. "He never drove it, did he? And Damon drives good. He just knows how to handle a car and nobody never showed him."

"And he knows how to pinch things, too."

"Prove it!"

"I don't have to prove it!" Mrs Bassie gave a laugh that was almost merry. "Seven cartons of soft pink toilet paper and a crate of malt vinegar, under his bed. Didn't take the cops long, did it? They'll put him away this time and good job, too."

"He might get probation."

"Not a chance. He's in breach of his last probation order."

Annette pleated the knee of her dress between her fingers.

"When they hear about the baby, they might let him off."

"And that's another thing. You can't have it."

Annette said nothing at all. After a

brief interval, long slow tears slid down her face and plopped on to her hands and knees.

"Did she say it? Mrs Berry?"

"Yeh. I flung a Coke tin at her, didn't I? Doesn't alter what she said. It would be bad for your mental and physical health if you went ahead and had it."

"Sounds as though you've swallowed a bleeding dictionary," said Annette. "If I want to have it, I should be allowed to. Nobody should be allowed to stop it."

"And who's going to bleeding keep it?" demanded Mrs Bassie. "How am I ever going to save up for Majorca, if you keep on falling with a kid?"

★ ★ ★

"It'll be all right, Annette," said Caroline Berry, soothingly. She had driven the girl to the hospital because Mrs Bassie had refused to go with her. She had left Simon asleep in bed. Last night, they had been to a party and she had met a marvellous man from the London School of Economics. She had gone to bed with him in an upstairs room. She did not

94

know if Simon knew.

Annette was very pale and a crop of little spots freckled her chin. Her dyed hair peaked out in front, so that she looked like a seedy, groggy chicken straight from the shell.

They sat in the hospital ante-room. Annette with her over-night bag on her knee.

"There'll be other babies. When you're older. When you've had time to grow up yourself and to know whether Damon is the right person to share your life with."

"He is."

They looked at each other. At least, Caroline thought, we've established some kind of rapport. She even felt a sort of surprised respect for the girl.

"You have to be sure."

"Can you ever be that sure?"

The consultant came towards them beckoning to Caroline. He was very pink, an unattractive man with a thin mouth and very little hair.

"A word with you, Mrs Berry." Caroline entered his room. She had her notes with her and gave him the information he required. It came to her that he rather fancied her, that he was posturing, half flirting, trying to register with her. She permitted herself a grim half-smile.

"I must make a move, Mr Williamson. My day is hectic."

"Come and have a drink with Iris and me. We're open house Sundays."

"That would be nice."

She thought, a little wildly, blue eyes can look *hot*.

They went back along the corridor together to the ante-room. The chair that Annette had been sitting on was empty.

Caroline went all over the building, looking for her. She looked in her own car, thinking Annette might have taken refuge there.

She spoke to the janitor at the door. Yes, he said wheezily, a thin girl with blonde hair had walked out ten minutes ago. Quite casually. Nothing to make him suspicious.

Caroline began to laugh, shakily. She thought: If anyone says a word to me, I'll cry. Then she thought, forcefully: Let her go. If they ask me to chase her up, I'll refuse. The hell with them. I'm going home to Simon and I'm stopping taking the Pill.

She rode triumphantly home in the car, a little hysterical, but chiefly happy. So there, she thought. So there, world, so there.

5

Abercrombie's Wedding

LULU was eating a dry biscuit lying down and being bad-tempered about marrying Abercrombie.

"It'll help," he urged her. "Now get up slowly." She did, but still spewed. Looking at her pale, disagreeable face in the round Habitat mirror in the bathroom, she sighed for the blade-thin, confident Libber who had once said she would bring up any child she bore on her own. With visiting rights if the man behaved himself. How come she had said yes to Abercrombie?

She returned to the bedroom and glared at him. Down at the supermarket, somebody at times tied a West Highland terrier to the barrier outside, where it sat in distraught, tousled dignity, dark eyes bright with alternate defiance and pleading. Increasingly it had begun to remind her of Abercrombie, turning what

98

she had regarded as a sensible organ, her heart, to melting butter. It had been after one such melting moment that she had chickened out to the growing need to reproduce one or more Abercrombies of manageable stature all requiring the hair pushed out of their eyes.

Cursing, she had recognised that either *Spare Rib* was on the wrong tack or that a certain four-letter word bandied about in the mass-circulation women's mags was acquiring validation in her own experience. With Julie from the commune now mothering a master butcher's four in the suburbs and Caro breast-feeding in the Beeb canteen, white flags were popping up all over the place and well-maybes turning into a rout.

"Buffets," Lulu spat at the hapless Abercrombie. "Flowers, photographs, your mother and this strange man she's bringing. My mother in her ghastly hat. I can't bear it."

"What would you rather we did?" he asked patiently. "Grab two people off the street for witnesses and do it on our own? Or not bother at all? You said — "

"Never mind what I said," whined

99

Lulu. "I'm all mixed up. If I don't marry you, you'll have no wife standing next to you the next time the Queen goes to the Beeb."

"You need a cuddle," Abercrombie diagnosed. It seemed his diagnosis was correct. He administered the treatment, promised to have a swift haircut for the ceremony the next day and went off to conduct his current affairs programme on which Lulu was sometimes the researcher.

She looked with grudging admiration at the delicate curve of her stomach. Try as she would to disregard it, she could not help a sensation of bumptious superiority. Together they had done this and it had all been so easy. They were obviously going to be very good at it. Thinking of Rembrandt, she made up her mind that if it were a girl, and it had better be, they would almost certainly call it Saskia.

Meanwhile Abercrombie's mother — she who gentle readers will remember from a previous story had pretended for thirty-six years to be his aunt, lies and falsification being more acceptable to her Calvinist nature than the admission of illicit passion — Abercrombie's mother Jean was on her way south by train for the ceremony bringing in tow the mysterious stranger Lulu had referred to in her matutinal gripings.

"I shall call you Alexander in front of the English," Jean informed the stranger now, passing him a cheese sandwich. "They wouldn't understand the name Eck. Don't thump your chest when you boak, or mention Ally Macleod, or pick your teeth with your Biro. You're standing in for the Abercrombies so be on your dignity."

The stranger gave her a swift uneasy smile, strangled at birth as the hard cheese fought for passage past his Adam's apple. He was a small, neat man with a remote blue eye, shaved close to the bone (the man not the eye), a wide new cap — designated a doolander (landing space for doves or pigeons) in the douce artisan milieu whence he sprang — decorously poised above generous ears.

Beneath an articulated tweed jacket that looked as though it had once accommodated most of the Eighth Army he wore dense, mud-coloured cords and on his lap nursed like the Holy Grail a raincoat, badge and shield of the wandering Scot.

"Now that he knows I'm his mother and not his auntie," Jean went on, "Archibald is dead set on finding out who his daddy is. And I don't feel like talking about it, Eck, not after all this time. So just sing dumb, Eckie. Lulu'll be after you too, to spill the beans. Just button your lip. You're my escort. I've told them you're a distant relative. That's all they need to know."

The rest of the journey passed happily enough as Jean showed the rest of the compartment the many snapshots of Archibald in her handbag, ranging from the Sunday School outing to Troon when he was six to an auspicious occasion at the Beeb with Archibald peering cautiously round a shoulder that belonged to Mr Ian Trethowan.

"He's a laddie to be proud of," Eck assured the dazed travellers, who had all begun to find things of immense interest on the other side of the window.

"And now he's settling down to

married life and I'm going to be a grannie," said Jean mistily. "I never thought to see the day."

After the brief register office ceremony the next day, Eck realised fully why Jean Abercrombie had been so anxious he should accompany her. He was of course famous at home for his social *sang froid*, be it at Pensioners' Hogmanay Dinner, Co-op Grand May Day Gala (Bring Own Mug) or Burns Night, but it was going to take all his prowess to meld this hard-boiled lot into proper celebrants of the wedding, prepared to sing *Flower of Scotland* and cry into their trifles as well-meaning friends should.

Abercrombie's flat had been transformed with flowers and food for the reception and bottles popped with gratifying regularity. Nonetheless, Eck felt sadly the lack of a good Co-op purvey and live fiddle and accordion instead of some thin, foreign tune on the record-player. Most of the guests were holding their glasses up as if they were test-tubes and they were testing for something nasty. At home, all the men would have been in proper blue suits, like him, and the women in big pink hats, with even the weans in new squeaky shoes with the price still stuck to the soles.

Here it was faded jeans, dusty corduroy, tee shirts and bedraggled long skirts and most of them looked as though they'd be all the better for the forcible feeding of a good mutton pie. He had heard someone say that Jean looked like a kidney-shaped dressing-table, but personally he liked a woman hung about with a few beads, handbag and corsage. Anything else looked plain uninviting.

"Have you been to London before, Mr Macmurtrie?" said a genteel small voice beside him, and Eck looked approvingly under the shady reaches of a big cream hat for its source.

"Only the wonst, when we beat youse at Wembley."

"I would have thought we had heard the last of that, after the World Cup." Eck looked appreciatively at Lulu's mother, for it was she, discreet Purley vowels and all. The gibe had been delivered as delicately as wee Dalglish netting a goal on one of his good days.

"When is she expecting it?" He headed back the conversational ball, indicating Lulu. Her floaty dress was Empire line, blatantly emphasising the fairly urgent nature of the exchange of promises. "Oh, not for ages." Lulu's mother stabbed him several times with small, venomous glances. "Doesn't she look sweet? Like a small Dresden shepherdess."

"Aye. Waiting for the lambing."

Lulu's mother came so close that Eck was sheltered under the mushroom hat. He could see a minute crumb of flaky pastry tremble like chaff on a bleached hair at the corner of her mouth.

"What we all would like to know," she whispered sweetly, "is a little more about Archibald's background. Do *you* know who his father was, Mr Macmurtrie? Why the great secret?"

Eck sucked in his breath reproachfully. "Oh, that would be family matters, Missus. Jean there is a reserved sort of woman, highly thought of in the Co-op Women's Guild and the WI. If she doesn't choose to disclose her affairs, I would never make so bold, neither." Blandly he met the suddenly

105

basilisk eye. "Could I have the pleasure of this dance?"

"What dance?" asked Lulu's mother nervously.

With a civil nod in Lulu's father's direction, Eck appropriated hat and wearer and swept both round in gracious circles, to a small murmur of applause. "No wedding without dancing," he pronounced. To a silently contemplative Beeb reporter near the record-player, he issued the firm instruction: "Turn it up, Jimmy, and grab haud of a lassie."

"That was a Household Name," reproved Lulu's mother. But to her surprise she was quite enjoying the exercise. Cyril never danced, and every now and then, when she was cleaning the house to Radio Two, she moved trance-like with a mop remembering a carefree, halcyon youth at the Lyceum before she had been caught up with Cyril's fertiliser. "You're a wee bobby-dazzler," whispered Eck approvingly in her ear, leading her into Nijinsky-like scissor-movements that stirred Terpsichore in her like honey. Cyril had joined the Household Name for a mutual glower.

Lulu had observed the manoeuvre. Picking petals from her posy, she said to Abercrombie, "Mother's nobbled Jean's little friend. You know what that means.

"Jean wouldn't have brought him had he been the sort to give anything away." He glanced over at his mother, holding court with a group of young acolytes. "She's enjoying her little mystery. Let her."

"Doesn't it worry you?"

"Not as much as it would worry me if I thought I was harassing her. She has her own reasons for silence."

"You're so well adjusted it's just incredible. Why haven't you any hang-ups? You should have."

"Can't be bothered." He shifted from one foot to the other.

"It could be him. I mean, Eck could be your father."

"If he is, it'll all come out in good time." He gave a suddenly lecherous grin. "Hey, Mrs Abercrombie, will it still be as nice now it's legal?"

Lulu came near to blushing, whether from vexation or embarrassment wasn't clear. Holding hands, they moved closer to Jean. She was telling her listeners how to make haggis. "You take the entrails of a sheep," she was saying. A man from *Panorama* was going pea-green, either from the haggis details or a hasty ostrich-like swallowing of six chicken vol-au-vents in a row. A more stout-hearted radio producer was leading Jean on, saying she ought to be on Woman's Hour.

After an hour or two, when the wine had done its work, the party was much more in line with Eck's hopes and expectations. A Young Writer of Promise had produced a penny whistle, while someone else had improvised a drum. The top of the battered piano the key of which Abercrombie had deliberately mislaid had been forced open and a Pole from World Service was picking out a tune on the yellowed keys.

Two studio managers were trying to remember the steps of a Greek dance. A Foreign Correspondent sang in the clear ringing tones of Oxon Academe a rough Scots bothy song that ended "Come take me in your arms, love, and blow the candle out", and a rosy girl journalist complied with the first part of the injunction.

"Here, son, what do they cry your name?" Eck asked the middle-aged Pole at the piano.

"Wadislaw," said the man. "Wally to you, if you like."

"Well, here, Sanilav, can you play any Scotch tunes? Any of the old yins with a swing, for dancing?"

"Like this?" With great good humour the Pole began a hammed-up version of *Loch Lomond*. With a sentimental tear in his eye, Eck went up to Jean, bowed and said formally, "Are you dancing?"

"Are you asking?" she coquetted.

"Yes, I'm asking."

"Then I'm dancing."

Small man and large woman somehow achieved a rhythmic cohesion that avoided disaster. Encouraged, the Pole swung into more music in the same vein and caught up in the mood of Lowland bacchanal, exponents of free-style disco dancing opted instead for holding each other and going round in circles.

Eck became aware of a stiffening in Jean's body. When twice she had brought her lace-ups firmly down on his instep, he said concernedly, "What's up, hen? Do you want to sit down?"

"That chap," she said, "at the piano. Did you say he was a Pole? He can play Scotch tunes like a native." Her face had gone pink with consternation, puffy with agitation. "Here, I think I know him. Take me over to him."

Eck accomplished the introductions and before he had finished Jean demanded of the Pole, "Were you in Scotland during the war? A wee village called Grumgavel? With the Free Poles?"

On his feet, the Pole clicked his heels and bowed assent.

"You used to play the piano in the Forces' canteen. I went there to make dried egg omelettes for the troops."

The Pole's face lit up. "Ah, yes? The Scots they were so kind. But I do not remember you, madam — "

"Well, no, you wouldn't. I had golden hair then, curly like Ginger Rogers — "

"Are you all right, Jean?" Eck was aware of something disquieting happening, something unforeseen. Jean looked as though she had just been hit by a bus and was rapidly going into shock. He pushed a chair under her, interposing himself between her and the Pole. "What's up?"

She pushed him aside, unwilling to take her eyes off the pianist for a second.

"You remember a thin chap — he came from Cracow. They called him Nosey because he had this long nose and he always looked so — so dejected."

"You are speaking of — wait a moment — I have it — Stepan Wojek I think it might have been. He got his number in the Italy campaign. Poor chap. He was always cold. Could that be the same?"

"Yes." Jean nodded. She was calmer now. "He was a married laddie and he missed his folks so much. He told me all about them. He was nice when you got to know him. Not really sad at all. Kind and nice and a good man, when all was said and done." She looked up from her handkerchief and saw that Lulu and Abercrombie were standing behind the pianist and had heard all she said.

There was a very long silence before the Polish pianist said, "It is all a long time ago, not so? And this should be a jolly wedding."

In the kitchen, Lulu supplied Jean with a hunk of kitchen tissue. The lace handkerchief had proved totally inadequate when they brought her out from the crowd and made her a strong cup of tea. Across the table, Eck watched her as carefully as a cat stalking a bird.

Abercrombie put his arm round his mother and said "It was him, wasn't it? Nosey. Stepan. He was my father?"

"I could never catch his name," Jean sniffed woefully. "How could I tell you there was this big, cold man called Nosey and he was your daddy? You would have thought it downright careless of me, not getting it right."

"We'll sort all that out now," he promised. He met Lulu's bright, warm gaze and then Eck's.

"Did you know?" he demanded.

"I knew most of it," Eck admitted. "Your mammy told me about it one afternoon we were at the Darby and Joan. It doesn't make any difference to my feelings about her."

"Is he really a distant relative?" demanded Lulu loudly.

Eck looked at Jean, at the floor and

out of the window. Then coyly back at Jean.

"It's for her to say."

Jean was looking more her old robust self already. "No. He's not a relative. I just didn't want any scandal talked about us."

"What is your relationship, then?" pursued Lulu sternly.

"He digs my tattie patch."

"She sews on my buttons. We're partners for the Valeta competition at the Over-Sixties." Eck and Jean exchanged supportive glances.

There was a worried, tentative expression on Jean's face as she looked up at Abercrombie. Something she saw there must have reassured her, for she suddenly found the formula she had been seeking.

Relaxing, patting her hair in a rare vain gesture, she spoke the words of the world-weary sophisticate everywhere.

"Me and Eck," she said finally, "is just good friends."

6

Starter Homes

FASHIONS came and went in the starter homes.

First there were perpendicular blinds, then the ruched sort, the hanging baskets of fuchsia and geraniums at the gable end, then garage doors painted in pastel colours, then driveways laid with bricks or cobbles rather than tar macadam.

They were called starter homes because you could secure one for a low deposit and the mortgages were just about feasible if both of you worked. And the fashions mattered because all the home-owners were young and liked to think of themselves as trendy — indeed, they did not know any other way of living. They were material girls and the boys who did their best to live up to them. *Young executives.* They had company cars and went on trips abroad and were computer literate. Their parents said they did not know how to wait for things, they were used to instant gratification. But they knew their own insecurities in the starter homes and keeping up with each other imposed its own strains.

It wasn't till the gilt had worn off the gingerbread a little and the starter homes had become places you lived in, came back to, had babies in, spilled food in, wallpapered, rowed in, rather than dead ringers for Habitat; had, in fact, become homes instead of show-places, that the three couples at the end of Jonquil Close realised how actually *content* they were, most of the time. There would always be rivalries, but Susan and Keith, Jane and Philip, Joss and Annie were *friends*.

The men now had jobs they had the measure of; the women had children to bring up. They knew all the idiosyncrasies of the local shops, where to get the best fish and vegetables, and which teachers were stroppy at the local infant school. The little girls went to dancing lessons. The small boys played at star wars. Plants established themselves in what had once been rubble-strewn starter gardens, trees flourished. The women baby-sat for each other, held coffee mornings. The men played golf. In other words, the starter homes and starter marriages matured and getting and spending took their place in the scheme of things. It did not matter so much to have fancy blinds once a kitten or two had made with the claws on them and garage doors were painted less often — what was the use when trikes and bikes chipped the paintwork? Perfect lawns were a little less perfect once football had been played on them and dogs had performed on them.

And the people you had competed with, realised Susan and Keith, and Jane and Philip, and Joss and Annie, were your friends and neighbours, who'd seen you with 'flu, in childbirth blues, in too much drink. Had waited with you for news in times of crises, gossiped with you on leisurely Sunday mornings, made up with you after stupid little differences about children bicycling and balls in flower-beds.

As the girls said, and meant, it would take a lot to break up the far end of

116

Jonquil Close. They really needed each other. They helped each other. The hard-edged rivalries of the earlier days, the starter days, were behind them. They had got back some of the closeness, the famous neighbourliness, of the days their parents and grandparents talked about, when women had worn clogs to t'mill and the lamplighter had done his rounds and no one had heard of Thatcherism or the market economy.

So there they were. Little fair Susan, with her designer spectacles and hand-knitted jumpers and liking for Michael Jackson, her light hand for pastry; and Keith, wizard-sharp with the computers he sold, quiet when teased about his small stature, happiest propagating orchids in his greenhouse.

They had two daughters, Lisa and Nanette.

And Jane and Philip. Jane, still working part-time at her physiotherapy, with her straight, sturdy broad-beamed build, her liking for unsuitable high heels, her rather splendid mane of kinky, permed hair and penchant for perfume; and Philip, quiet, a little inaccessible, a good do-it-yourself man, given to oaths and bad grammar, his main soft spot his son, Barnaby.

Joss and Annie had three children, two girls and a boy, named Cherry, Scarlett and Sam. Annie's mother said childbirth for Annie was like popping peas. Everybody liked Annie, who was gentle and soft-spoken but a great manager. Her children were nicely mannered. Sometimes she looked tired but she always smiled. Joss was a neat and particular man, whose thin moustache swooped up endearingly when he laughed and whose dark eyes almost disappeared in their fans of side-wrinkles. He was a man with a good presence and a liking for reading maps and encyclopedias.

These assorted people led a contented and structured existence, something many people still do, if you can bring yourself to ignore the bleatings and socio-criticism of the daily press. They had learned that children are the glue of family life, that kisses can mean more than new clothes, that a familiar footstep, the ring of a known voice, can mean more than promotion or commendations from the boss or the latest three-piece suite. (These things have to be said, at the risk of ridicule and the accusation of sentimentality, because people have forgotten they are true.) If the girls were close and neighbourly, the men had an easy camaraderie. They played sports together, took their children swimming together, drank lager together, loaned each other lawn-mowers, passed on to each other the latest dirty story and, if they argued, did so good-naturedly.

They were united in something else. They believed, even if it was only at some deep, subliminal level, in keeping women in their place. They would have denied this instantly if you had charged them with it, but then there would have been a shuffling of feet and an avoidance of eye contact while one or other vouchsafed that women were 'weaker' or 'softer' or 'needed looking after', or 'had the kids to think about'.

The women colluded. "My husband wouldn't like it," they would say, when they wanted to get out of something. They put their husbands forward as arbiters of whether they should have a job, where the children should go to school, how they should vote, or dress, or do their hair. They would look flirtatious and smiling as they did this, as if they were poor helpless little pawns on the chessboard where their menfolk were knights and kings. This was the basis on which they had been given the wedding ring: if you were too independent, men shied away. Getting married in the second half of the twentieth century depended on how far you compromised on feminist principles.

"You've got to watch women," the men told each other. If you didn't, they would have you doing all the washing-up, they would have you taking charge of the kids at the weekends, they would spend all their time gossiping, going to slimming and aerobic classes and leaving you no time for getting it down. Lager, that is.

It was all done very good-humouredly. Joss and Philip and Keith invented for the purpose of their strategy something called the Steady Men's Union. Steady Men did not give 'the wife' her breakfast in bed unless she was really under the weather. They did not go in for the buying of flowers or chocolate except on a rarity basis — after a serious fall-out, or an exceptionally heavy bevvy, say.

They were never too lavish with compliments or ready to undertake 'female' tasks like bringing in the washing if it rained and had keen definitions of women's work — all cooking, cleaning, changing of beds, etc. Anything grimy or awkward, naturally.

Too much attention to wifely whims meant threat of expulsion from the Union. Steady Men had at all times to keep an eye on the war between the sexes and make sure that no ground was ever given that could not be got back.

The starter homes had lost any pretence of newness, had begun to show the first signs of neglected, peeling paintwork, and the occasional slightly overgrown garden, when a startling thing happened in Jonquil Close.

Joss fell devastatingly in love with his wife, Annie.

Those who have never been wed will be unfamiliar with this strange phenomenon. The fact is, the start of a marriage is not necessarily the point at which a couple are most in love. In most marriages, periods of calm and acceptance, even periods of distaste and estrangement, are followed by a repetition, even a heightening, of the initial bliss. Marriage is never an even graph.

And the reasons for the startling leap in Joss's graph? A life-threatening illness, through which Annie nursed him devotedly. Her buying of a particular nightie, an *extremely* delectable nightie, one could even say a rather naughty nightie, once he was better. The shedding of certain chubby curves on her part and her metamorphosis into a slender Atalanta who could wear the latest styles with a rare confidence. And finally, the Little Job she had acquired, now the children were settled in school, and at which she was a lot better and more proficient than she let on (and through which she was to rise eventually to executive status, though that is another story).

Suddenly, Joss could not get enough of her. He was sharing her now with the outside world, as she had always had to do with him. She was amusing and interesting and busy and there was just the chance some other bloke would think so too.

The other chaps in the Steady Men's Union looked at him askance. He was taking Annie out at least once a week to dine in posh restaurants (while one of the other wives baby-sat, for goodness' sake). If given the opportunity of a game of golf with his pals, or a visit to some recommended pub, he would cash in his chance for the sake of a night at home watching the telly with — and please note this, — not '*the* wife', but '*my* wife'. 'My wife Annie'.   He was frequently seen to be bearing home a bunch of flowers on the back seat of his car and observed coming out of Thornton's the chocolate shop with an extravagant box of chocs with a ribbon round it. (The rule was if you bought your wife chocolates it was in a quarter-pound bag and more likely to be mint humbugs than chocolates, because you liked mint humbugs and she had to think of her figure.)

None of these operations went unobserved. Susan was not the whiney sort but she did say pointedly to Keith one evening, "You don't spoil me in little ways, you know. Not the way Joss does Annie."

Keith had known what was coming and had his answer ready. He loved his wife, too, of course he did. She made his omelettes to a T and never let the soap go soggy in the wash-basin.

"I do pamper you, pet," he responded. "Only I do it in subtle ways. I don't like to be obvious." He was thinking of how he let her have the inside of the *Mail* at breakfast and the times he'd said nothing when she put cold feet on his in bed.

"They're so subtle they're undetectable," said Susan, with devastating accuracy. "You need a haircut, you do," she added sourly. "And I hate you in those new glasses. I'm getting a job."

Jane's approach was nothing like so head-on. She wanted a brother or sister for Barnaby and because this had not happened and because Philip was hard to talk to, she had grown plump and a little apathetic. She developed a skill in nagging she had never known she possessed.

"That front gate," she would apostrophise Philip the moment he entered. "If that were Joss's gate, it would be fixed instanter. Annie only has to say."

When the Steady Men met at their favourite hostelry, they tried all the usual tactics to bring Joss to his senses. Ribaldry, sarcasm, even, in Philip's case, downright plain speaking.

"If you give a lass a bit o' rope, she'll hang herself," he explained clumsily. "Now I'll do what my lass says, but not the direct minit she says it. Do it minit she opens her mouth, what are you? Nobbut a sidekick."

"Why keep her on the hook?" demanded Joss, now grown large and ugly as Female Chauvinist of this and every other year in his mates' eyes. "Why make it necessary for them to nag? They don't like nagging, any more than we like *being* nagged."

"Another pint, Sylvia?" said Philip brusquely. "Is it the lemonade shandies you're on, or do you want a diet coke with a cherry on?"

Jane sat in her doctor's surgery and wept. "Get a full-time job," said the doctor, who couldn't think of anything else to suggest. Jane found one in a sports and leisure club, where soon the gym instructor was promising to leave his wife for her, if she could bring herself to do the same to her husband.

The day she left what had been her starter home, Jane went round each room touching random pieces of furniture, a vase she liked here, a picture there. A lot of her had gone into the making of this home and what she would be without it terrified her deeply. She knew also she would have to leave her son with his father for she was to be cast in the role of scarlet woman. She would never have a home like it again.

Somewhere, somehow, they had taken a wrong turning. It had been hard to accept she would not have another child after Barnaby, but in the end she could have come to terms with it. She had let herself go to an extent that she was now doing her best to remedy and maybe if she had not, Philip would not have been so hard or so cold. Or had it been the other way round? If he had been less hard, more loving, would she have lost interest in how she looked? Now she would never know.

Susan got a job at the same time as Jane. As it was in a clothes shop she was able to develop her interest in fashion and after a time, she and another assistant set up on their own.

Susan became obsessed with clothes and dressed in a hard, immaculate fashion. She and her partner went to fashion fairs, indulged (as Keith now did) in splendid lunches and went to the theatre when they felt like it. They led the full business lives that women can nowadays. The two girls became adept at making their own meals and following their own interests. After a time, Susan suggested to Keith they should stop All That. When he asked her what she meant, she said she had gone off sex entirely, that it no longer mattered to her any more. But for sex, she really meant love and respect.

The starter homes emptied one by one. Joss and Annie moved into a larger house and had another daughter they named Amber. Philip moved back to his mother's with his son, Barnaby, while Jane took another lover after the gym instructor. Keith took a flat in town and pretended to the young women he took out occasionally that he was single, though he never bothered to formalise a divorce. Susan and the girls had a flat above the first of her fashion salons.

The starter homes which had begun so brilliantly looked a little more down-market now. Young couples starting out looked over them but came out with the corners of their mouths turned down. Eventually somebody bought them and sporadic efforts were made to smarten them up. They were a bit ordinary, truth to tell, and those who bought them led less than spectacular lives, and knew that the first rule of survival was to use the curtains you already had, and never to expect too much.

7

Back Payments

IRIS had not been prepared for the long siege of Charlie Chamberlain. The whole idea of getting in a decorator had been to avoid the protracted muddle and bad temper attendant on doing it yourself. Not that she hadn't wanted to. With her husband Grant away on a business trip to Australia it would have been as good a way as any of filling in the time till his return. But as she said to Agnes Wetherhead, what with her knee joints and the frozen shoulder she got whenever she painted anything above her head, this year it just wasn't on.

Also, although she had been a good social democrat for as long as she could remember (teachers' training college if not earlier) it now looked as though the whole thing were going out of fashion. It was the time of the Heavies. Before things got too out of kilter, she somewhat guiltily wanted to enjoy the money she and Grant had worked for, now the family had flown the coop. She thought of herself as a kind woman, whose kindnesses had been increasingly thrown back in her face. She had taught recalcitrant teenagers with lumpen shoes and sullen expressions right up till last year, when quite suddenly she had decided she had had enough. Now she wanted things done for *her*. She hankered after the old bourgeois delights like little dressmakers and workmen who didn't hector you and waitresses who cared whether your coffee was hot or not.

Half amused and half appalled, she thought she would probably end up like her mother. That crusted old reactionary had been a despot in shops and with those she regarded as servants but had ended up undeservedly loved and respected for it.

Maybe there was a lesson there somewhere. But she was certainly the reason why Iris had grown into what her disrespectful elder son called a pinko. Which she wasn't. She just didn't like to see people being put down.

Charlie Chamberlain had advertised in

the Village Post Office. 'Handy Man will tackle GUTTERS, FENCING, ALL INSIDE PAINTWORK'. She'd had a job getting hold of him. The phone number given had belonged to a sister-in-law who had made mysterious noises about seeing whether the gentleman in question would be available. Afterwards Iris realised the unorthodox nature of Charlie Chamberlain's labours. He probably paid no tax and might even have been on Social Security. It was with some misgivings, even then, that she started him off in the hall.

A small, leathery man in dirty white overalls and a flat cap, he turned up an hour late on the first day. When she remonstrated, his head snapped up, he looked aggrieved and Iris had the same sickening premonition of a war of attrition that she'd had at the start of an autumn term with 4B. He was late also on the following two days.

On the first morning there was an argument about the dado.

"Soon have that down," said Charlie. "Don't 'ave them no more, do they? Gone out of fashion, they have."

"I don't wish it down," said Iris, firmly.

"Do you in the buttermilk, all the way down."

"Chestnut brown for the lower half, please."

She kept the dado, but ended up in the kitchen panting with irritation while Charlie clearly sulked. His whistling stopped. All that could be heard was the slap-slap of the chestnut brown going on where he obviously felt it had no business to be. Iris took the dog for a walk and came back in a better frame of mind.

People like Charlie had known exploitation in the past. It was good to see a blossoming of working-class ego. Not that Iris classified people by class, as it were. Iris wanted to believe in a God that would rate even the humblest sparrow. But by thinking of Charlie as a sparrow, she knew she was guilty of condescension and worse, of sentimentality. When it was lunchtime she deliberately asked him to share the table with her, giving him the warm seat by the Aga, which he took without demur.

"I've warmed some good, nourishing soup for starters," she said. "If it won't put you off your sandwiches." A little embarrassed at the sucking noises he made against his spoon, she launched into a lively account of how she economised even with left-over quantities of soup now that she had installed a freezer.

"Wife's got two freezers." Charlie gave her a pitying stare, crossed his legs relaxedly and took out a between-course roll-up. "You and your hubby been down the new road-house yet?"

She had seen the Jags and Daimlers outside the converted farmhouse with its red neon signs advertising French and Italian cuisine. "Not our scene, I'm afraid."

"You want to get the old man to take you down there. All hunting scenes round the walls, lavs like the Taj Mahal. Took the wife and the two unmarried daughters down there Saturday. Had to wear formal, mind. Wife and daughters all in their la-di-dah bits, long gowns and them gold shoes with the narrow straps. Me in my mohair. Scampi, sparkling wine, big steaks, sweet off the trolley.

Cabaret. Dancing. After-dinner mints. The lot. Set me back. But worth it."

She knew he was being provocative, assertive, vulgar. He sat there, a small, shrunken man, prematurely bent with hard labour, his yellow tombstone teeth set wide apart by arbitrary extractions, his hands gaping with soda-and-turps-produced hacks, a childhood's deprivation evident in a hundred ways from glottal stops and adenoids to lank hair and dandruff. Defying her to feel sorry for him. She tried to picture him in his mohair, but couldn't. She did not know what she felt. Anger? Astonishment? Disbelief? Certainly curiosity.

"I didn't know people could afford that sort of thing," she said, as mildly as she could.

Charlie's cracked and nicotined lips parted in a reluctant leer. "There's ways, my gel," he said, touching the side of his nose with his forefinger. "Ways. What's it all about if you ain't got a bit of style?"

Iris sprang up, leaving him to his filthy preoccupation with stubbing out his roll-up on her china side-plate.

She wanted style, all right. Tiffany lamp-shades, sinful fat cushions, a glass and chromium tea trolley, the house refurbished from top to bottom. Yet a lifetime of non-conformist thrift prevented her. Grant and she had bought everything to last and money should be used providently. Later that afternoon she wrote out a cheque for Oxfam, enough to start a water well in India, and felt better, more able to cope with Charlie's sudden outbreaks of song or whistling, that started out as though they meant to be tunes but ended up in formless humming.

It was after lunch that Iris felt the chips were down and they knew each other. If she had half hoped for deference, it was clearly not forthcoming. But neither would she give in to his intransigence over colour-schemes. When she wanted duck-egg blue in the sitting-room, he beat her about the head with the eau-de-nil adopted on his advice by the Paki woman who had moved into the new Regency by the park.

She held her ground about that and about the sparkling white rather than burnt orange woodwork in the bathroom. He sulked, but as she treated his tantrums with a sunny indifference he began to allow a guarded respect for her opinions. It was funny, she thought. In a strange way they were growing used to living together. She slopped three teaspoonsful of sugar into his morning coffee with bland abandon. He turned up on time and wiped his feet on the front doormat.

Occasionally, instead of having sand-wiches for lunch, he sloped off to one of the village pubs and came back in a cheerful mood. Once she was sure he was drunk. He swung on a plank above the well of the staircase, singing something that started off as *In The Mood* and ended up as *The Battle-Hymn of the Republic.* Petrified, she wondered what she would do if he fell off. He didn't, of course, but he went home early, a little shamefaced and, she suspected, more than a little hung-over.

Perhaps in order to mollify her, he brought next morning the first of the gifts. Half a pound of smoked salmon. One day she had let slip it was the one luxury food she lusted after.

"I can't take this, Mr Chamberlain."

Iris's pink morning face shone with embarrassment, but he pushed the packet back towards her across the kitchen table, making the now-familiar gesture of the forefinger to the side of the nose, and accompanying it by a leering wink and alarming grimace. Rather than go through the whole pantomime again, she put the salmon in the fridge and later found herself buying new brown bread and lemon to go with it, almost without a pang of conscience.

"Like it, did you?" asked Charlie the next day. "I can get you anything in the food line." He cupped his right hand low and swung it behind his back, to indicate the nefarious nature of any such transaction.

"I wouldn't ask you," said Iris, terrified.

"They all does it, love," said Charlie. "At the hotel where my youngest gel works. Run by British Rail, it is, so you could say it belongs to us, the people, the rate-payers."

At this piece of sophistry, Iris paled and

felt faint. The next day, Charlie brought her a two-kilo packet of sugar (scarce then because of some strike somewhere) and a round Irish fruit-cake in a tin box.

"No. Thank you all the same. Please take it away with you." Iris hoped she sounded as firm as she intended. She did not look at the offending items on the table.

"No cause for worry." Finger to nose. "That lot ain't from the hotel. They're from the wife's supermarket, where she works. Little thank-you for the kindnesses you've shown me. Sugar in me coffee and all that. The wife is never one to take a kindness for granted." When Iris had a piece of the cake later, it tasted absolutely delicious; made, as the tin box claimed, with All Butter.

Taking Tigger, the boxer, over the copse and round by the golf course, Iris wondered a little wildly what was happening to her. Was it some middle-aged softening of the brain? Was she missing Grant's stolid, *Guardian*-principled presence more than she'd bargained for? What a pity she feared flying and had not been able to accompany him to Australia, where she could have visited her second cousin Margaret in Melbourne.

By the time Tigger had sniffed up a Pekinese and had had a fight with an Airedale, she had regained some of her composure. She must accept no further gifts from Charlie. No matter how tempting. No matter how insidious.

And she'd have to tell him to get a move on. He was way behind schedule, mainly because he knocked off for a chat whenever he felt like it, or wandered out for a mid-morning pint on the pretext that he needed more Polyfilla or paint thinner.

He was arrogant, amoral, with awful tales of his delinquent children who did ton-ups on their motor-bikes, got into fights with knives at the village hall and fell heedlessly into the family way. Some member of the family or other was always in running battle with the council/police/education authority/-probation service. And yet the truth was she had become quite horribly fascinated by him, by this way of life so totally foreign to her own.

And in his warped way he was

generous. When she broke her reading glasses, he brought a caseful containing a hundred or more spectacles, all with expensive frames, and she was sorely tempted to pick a blue tinted pair that seemed to fit her prescription. It appeared a distant cousin of his wife, with a college education and a mortgage, was as bent (or, as Charlie saw it, as enterprising) as the rest. Iris thought of Russia where, it was said, fiddling had become a way of life.

It was as Grant's return date drew nearer and the Irish fruit-cake was finally finished that Iris began to draw about her her somewhat tattered moral scruples. She had a long, uplifting chat with her friend Agnes Wetherhead about the guiding role Britain still had to play in world affairs and having resisted the temptation of the tinted specs felt in a stronger position to harangue Charlie Chamberlain.

The opportunity came when he had finished scraping down the kitchen walls, ready for the last onslaught of paper-hanging. While she brewed up a strong pot of tea, he nudged his head towards the hall.

"What you need there now is a nice bit of tobacco-brown carpeting."

It was exactly what she had been thinking. The turkey red was still good, not in the least threadbare, but she suddenly hated it with a strength of loathing that surprised her.

She said, sharp and sour, "There's nothing wrong with the carpet already there."

"Got just the one for you." Charlie stirred his tea benignly. "Lovely length of tobacco-brown shag. Lying in me shed doing nothing. We done the house out in it before Shirl's wedding." He showed his yellow teeth in what he felt to be a charming smile. "Don't arsk me where it come from, that's all. Know what I mean?"

"Oh, I do." She threw down her teaspoon. "Look, you won't get away with this kind of thing forever, Mr Chamberlain. And it really won't do. I have a friend, a Miss Wetherhead, head of a large comprehensive school, and she says the country must start now on moral revival or we're down the plug-hole. Now I do agree with her. Thieving, fraud, violence, all kinds of petty chicanery — no, it really isn't good enough, Mr Chamberlain. You must see you should be showing your children an example."

He sucked his tea reflectively. Tried balancing his spoon on the edge of his cup. Looked at the ceiling. Gave her a grave, forgiving smile.

"Trouble was, who showed me? My old woman, she sold everything for the drink. Me dad, he got shot to pieces in the Kaiser's bit of bovver, didn't he? And I done me bit in the larst. You gotta take out of life what you can, gel. Only got the one time round. Know what I mean?"

"I don't mean to suggest you are not a brave man," Iris said, with dignity, realising that she probably meant it. "But I think you are a very dishonest one." She rushed out into the garden, her face pink, and brought in the morning's washing. She knew things could not be the same again. No more trophies, no more songs on the step-ladders. Mr Chamberlain papered the kitchen in silence and the next day presented his bill. It was for a hundred pounds more than the estimate.

Iris practised her yoga relaxation exercises before she confronted the decorator.

"I think the sum we agreed was four hundred and fifty pounds, Mr Chamberlain."

Charlie Chamberlain raised a basilisk eye. "Gone over me time, haven't I? Walls was worse than I thought they would be."

"If you have gone over your time, it is because you were tempted down to the flesh-pots in the village of a morning."

"Ho no. That was supplies."

"Supplies of draught beer. Guinness. Whatever it is you pour down your insatiable throat."

"I don't like no bovver," said Charlie. "Neither do me sons."

Iris shivered. She had seen the sons.

"I'll pay you fifty pounds extra. Not a penny more."

"Make it seventy-five and we'll call it quits." He looked at her with an almost merry irony. She paid up.

He had piled his battered boards and ladders into a broken-down anonymous van when Iris summoned up enough courage to call him back. Her legs were trembling so much she thought they were going to buckle under her.

"That tobacco-brown shag. The carpet. In your shed. You did say I could have it."

His look was long, measuring, almost derisory. Then "Right, gel," said Charlie Chamberlain, without animosity. "I'll get Brian to bring it up in the dark."

She had to admit it looked lovely when it was down. It went right up into all the corners, under the umbrella stand and there was enough for the downstairs loo. It made the house look trendy, luxurious. The way she wanted it to look. She even stopped lusting after the Tiffany lamps.

Grant liked the carpet very much, but she decided not to explain the circumstances of its acquisition to him. It would only set up all kinds of recriminatory vibes between them. In her own mind there were blurry boundaries when she went over the moral arguments.

She should not have taken the carpet. Or the cake. Or the sugar or the salmon. But she had, she had. Out there was the jungle and she could hear the jackals cry.

8

Sweet Milk Scone
Meets Godzilla

YOU'RE the same as us, my English friends tell me reassuringly. What with Marks and Sparks and Next and Principle's in all the towns, what's the differences between England and Scotland? (This has been one of the main enigmas of my life — the difference, I mean.) What with watching the same television programmes, and all this going abroad, and packet food, paella for the masses, there isn't any (difference, they mean).

Well, they wouldn't call a person a Sweet Milk Scone in England. They wouldn't call a person a scone, for a start. They might call him a milksop, or a weakling, or a wally, or a bit of a pansy, but none of these words has quite the right daikie connotation. Here I see I am getting into ever-deeper water. All

146

right, daikie means doughy, or lacking in spirit, and if you want to see what we have lost in supple, evocative terms I commend to you the Dictionary of the Older Scottish Tongue, or the Concise Scottish Dictionary will do. (What else we have lost and why we will always be different belongs elsewhere.) His name was David but when he walked into the little baker's in the Lowland town they said: here comes The Sweet Milk Scone. This was because whatever else he asked for, he always included a request for one such item. When his mother had been alive it had been two sweet milk scones, which they ate for their tea with a scrape of butter and some of her home-made jam.

But after her death, it was just one sweet milk scone and the shop assistants snickered and smirked as they tossed the small paper bag in a parabola between the thumb and forefinger of each hand, screwing up each end, and handed the tea-time dainty over the counter with a request for the requisite number of pence. We have to allow for boom-flation. Once it cost two pence per scone. Now it is more like twenty pence.

I have to say that their mild mocking of the man called David was not unqualified by respect. He was a man who always dressed respectably. He had good flannel trousers and a neat checked jacket for the summer months and in the winter he wore a decent overcoat and felt hat, with well polished brown brogue shoes and good leather gloves which he carefully did up at the wrist, after putting the change from his purchases away in a worn and unexceptional flat leather purse. He had a job at the council offices which he carried out conscientiously and well.

But his main fault was that he was too agreeable, or to be more precise, was ready to agree with anything anybody said, sometimes even before anything *was* said. If he met a matron in the street, on her way for her pension or some embroidery threads and she offered non-committally, "It's a nice day, Davie," because she had gone to the same women's guild as his mother, he would reply, "It's an awf'y nice day, Mrs MacAusland. As nice a day as we're likely to get. We're the lucky ones, are we not, Mrs MacAusland?" and this with much bowing and taking off of hats and smiling and nodding and side-stepping on the pavement, so that Mrs MacAusland proceeding on her way for her pension or her embroidery threads felt she had (a) been summarily assaulted by a wet-mouthed, over-enthusiastic Labrador or (b) been hit sideways on the head by a soggy cushion.

Or supposing he met a professional nonagenarian, of whom there were several in the town, for the air was fresh and beneficial, he would listen patiently to their complaints against youth, change or the Health Service and their catalogue of minor, specific ailments before asking, "How's your general health?"

It was generally lowered before he took leave of these senior citizens, for he had exhausted them with his well-meaning catechising and over-solicitous comments.

Do not ask David to have opinions of his own. He holds only what you own, he will never vouchsafe any argument because to do so would shake his universe to its foundations.

It is useless to speculate as to why the man called David had adopted such a downtrodden attitude, one that made it easy for little girls in bakers' shops to feel his superior. (There were wags in the town who suggested that if you said to him 'The Clyde is flowing backwards this morning,' David would have agreed with them; not only that — he would have added that he had always suspected this might happen.) There is in a nation that paid lip-service to the lairds a certain vein of servility that may not yet have withered or dried up. But there is also a genuine desire to please, to make all things well, that is born of a generosity of spirit. My great-aunt made me open the front-door wide when greeting visitors, saying anything else was an insult. My grandmother fed beggars at the door. In the thirties, my Micawber-like uncle would give me, a mere schoolchild, the last silver threepenny from his waistcoat pocket if he met me in the street. Contrary to the wiseacres, we are not a miserable race and the harsh morality we learned from Knox makes us genuine advocates of fair play.

150

So David's transmutation into The Sweet Milk Scone could have begun with the wish to placate and please his widowed mother, Maggie. He may have slipped into it from the unprepossessing angle of his nose or the fact that his ears stuck out and his voice sounded catarrhal.

I don't know — I am not a psychologist, only the writer. And if you, the reader, are a sophisticated and travelled city person, I hope you will make allowances for small-town mores, for mothers (not only in Scotland) who manipulate their children's feelings by threats and sulking, not looking for these attitudes to be taken seriously, though they often are.

But in the end what makes one person tough and another soft is not necessarily predictable or explicable. David was as he was and coped with his life by propitiation.

★ ★ ★

Whereas Godzilla went at life like a tank.

Well, of course, she was no more Godzilla than he was The Sweet Milk

Scone. She was Robertina, the last three letters grudgingly added by her father when he had discovered, to his rage and surprise, that there was no way of changing his first and only child into the son he had desired. Him, a farmer, with the best bull in the county, to end up wi' a lassie, and his begrutten[1] wife stuck in the chimley-neuk, ailing from one sickness after another!

Again, I am no psychologist, but simple instinct tells me even Farah Fawcett Major would have ended up Godzilla, had she had the farmer for a father. Would have ended up in hairy, long-lasting tweeds and flat-heeled shoes, with a haircut like a lavvy brush and an expression that would curdle cream. As luck would have it, Robertina worked in the local Department of Health and Social Security, where hard-up claimants blamed her, often unfairly, for the strictures of the system, and where the nickname was born, and stuck.

Those she dealt with and who grew to

---

[1] tear-stained

dread her piggy, searching eye would have been surprised to know how Robertina-Godzilla longed for romance. All through her life she had waited for a man to come along who would realise her true worth and carry her off to his castle or council house — as the years passed, it mattered less where.

In her bedroom at home, there were careful piles of romantic tales, stories of quite ordinary girls who started off as nurses or shop assistants and ended up married to men with yachts who called you 'My darling one'. 'My darling one' she would respond in the dark of her room, while the best bull in the county bellowed in the field below. The less the likelihood of a man with a yacht coming along, the more crushing Robertina's daily encounters became. She berated street sweepers, bullied bus conductors, was a despot in shops and made a speciality of reporting telephone operators. Inside, she was this sweet, misunderstood girl who needed somebody's arms around her: outwardly she was a crusty dame with all the sex appeal of an armadillo.

All right. I know you are waiting for it. I am not telling you about The Sweet Milk Scone and then Godzilla for nothing. True. There must be some connection between the two — already the language is beginning to have a sexual connotation. You see how brain-washed you have become.

Well, the truth is they had been acquaintances and sort of friends for years. She had been a year ahead of him at the Academy, but their ages were the same because he had been held back by his adenoids. She remembered him jogging miserably round the playing field in long shorts and singlets and he could picture her whacking the life out of some innocent hockey ball, even then a big-busted girl with a stare that curled chip papers.

They had met at social events like whist drives and church soirees and were on easy bantering terms as they both entered the second half of the dangerous forties.

And then on a dull day in a dark December, they sat down opposite each other in Ellen Harker's Tearooms, both low in morale, both burdened by supermarket shopping and wet umbrellas.

It has to be said that what followed did so more out of desperation and depression than any romantic impulse. They agreed to go to the pictures together. He tried not to think of her piggy eyes and she kept her mind off the fact that his teeth overhung his lower lip more than she remembered. There were no illusions. Both realised that loneliness and existential angst had forced them into companionship. Any port in a storm. It was the first time either had had an assignation with a member of the opposite sex.

It was quite a successful outing. They saw some space odyssey or other and at the bus stop afterwards, the way he stood with his arm on the rail might easily have been mistaken for a wish to put it — his arm, that is, not the bus-rail — round her substantial waist. The wave he gave her as the bus pulled out was cordial enough to warm her all the way to the farm stop and she even answered her mother when that sorely-tried parent shouted a goodnight.

After that, there were other, more

ambitious outings, such as to the church's production of *The Mikado*, a trip to Glasgow, a visit to her great-uncle in an old folk's home and Sunday Special Lunch at the Caribbean Chicken Hotel and Motel. She bought a white blouse with frills and he invested in two new shirts from Burton's, with toning ties.

She never took anyone to the farm. Her father's brooding bad temper and rudeness made this impossible. So as the friendship . . . I was about to say warmed but that is not the expression I am seeking . . . shall we say as the friendship proceeded on its timorous and qualified way, he invited her to his council flat for a meal.

In this, he felt an unusual amount of quiet confidence. He could make quite a passable stew with dumplings and a custard without lumps to go over an apple crumble. His mother had been a relentless and perfectionist teacher even when unable to stir a pot or cut up vegetables herself.

He even had flowers on the table and paper napkins. He took Robertina's coat and put it away in the bedroom and

156

while he completed the cooking switched on News at Six for his guest to watch.

"This is very nice, David," she said, stretching out her feet towards the electric fire and feeling the strains of being shouted at and vilified in the office fade.

He came through from the tiny room his mother had always called the kitchenette, unselfconsciously wearing one of his late parent's frilly aprons and beamed at her approvingly.

"I miss seeing someone in that chair. All you need now is a piece of embroidery in your hand and the picture is complete."

"Maybe there should be a cat on the hearth," she suggested. "Apart from that — " she eyed the steaming stew he bore in appreciatively, "all this is very cosy."

"And there's wine," he said, forgetting to agree with her about the cat. "No expense spared, eh? Nothing but the best." And he drew the green and black curtains before the woman across the road could make out through her beige nets what was going on.

★ ★ ★

"Are you courting?" they asked her in the Department.

She did not know how to answer. In one way, it would be very sweet to hint that an engagement and a ring might not be very far off, to confound all their notions of her as a dyed-in-the-wool old maid.

But on the other hand there was David's image. In some ways he looked better since they had started going out together, but he still went around agreeing with everybody and being so ingratiating it sometimes made her feel physically sick.

She had tried bullying him out of it, but if anything it just made him worse. "You're right, I know." He nodded his head. "It's just the way I am." And he looked so dejected and apologetic she had given up. She had thought of saying to him, "You're not a bad-looking man. You've never broken the law. You hold down a decent job," of trying to build up his own estimation of himself. But the quality of ingratiation had become the man. It was almost as though he had to hang on to all the ceremonials of obsequiousness, that his fawning had the quality of compulsion.

In a strange way, she understood, for she still rose up from her bed at the farm and charged at life head-on, intolerance the only balm she had ever found for the hurts inflicted by being her father's child, for being ugly and badly shaped and never, ever, appreciated.

So she said nothing until the enquiries subsided. It was nobody's business what she and David intended.

They were two of a kind. Oddities. Flotsam on a sea of contemporary advice on how to make yourself over, be more attractive, be successful. Their loneliness had bred a kind of intransigence and resistance. When they were together they did not even bother to pretend.

"I'm fat and ugly," she told him on one occasion. "I'm like a big bolster that someone has tied carelessly in the middle. I have a face like the back of a cab." And for once he had said nothing, confounded by the strength of her feelings. He had produced a box of chocolates and helped

159

her to find the coffee cream.

On another occasion, she had listened while he told her about a cousin of his, with whom he'd been very friendly as a child. The cousin had gone to London, risen to the heights of the Civil Service, married a beautiful blonde and had four wonderful children. She had known this was a kind of threnody for his own lost opportunities, for he had made a point of saying he'd actually got higher marks than his cousin in class.

She'd wanted to shout at him, reproach him for being wet, but then, if he'd not been wet, he would have gone away and she would not now have the benefit of his company. Which was increasingly all she had to look forward to in the bleakness of her life.

So she did not say anything either. And there was something, a kind of contentment that verged on actual happiness, because there was no pretence, no hypocrisy, between them.

In that first year, since they had started seeing each other, her mother died. That frail, complaining, self-absorbed little woman, with her leg ulcers and bad heads, finally made it to the peaceful graveyard at the head of the valley. It looked as though her father would soon follow. The doctor had described it as an inevitability if he did not stop his now ferocious drinking and this he did not do.

Robertina said to David, "What shall I do? I can't stand it much longer at the farm. The stink and the mud are getting into my head. They never leave me."

"You could come here," he said. They were coffeeing at his flat.

"You mean — move in?"

"Why not?"

"I couldn't just — move in. It would have to be legal."

"All right. We could make it legal."

They had not discovered any physical means of expressing tenderness between them. He still saw women as a mystery. She still wanted a strong man with a moustache who would call her my darling one. But she thought she could live in his house and listen to his little, chattering voice, and let him cook sometimes and even do embroidery because he liked to see a woman sew.

"Would it work?" she asked, almost tremulously.

"The offer's on the table." He let his eyes meet hers, which even now he did not often do and she thought with pleasure that he'd learned about irony, he wasn't quite as sure-as-death as once he'd been. As to his teeth hanging over his lower lip, and the twist of his nose, it was amazing how unfortunate traits could be accepted when fudged by familiarity. You could even get to like them, because they were there.

"We don't need to rush anything," he said.

"No," she agreed.

But she came more and more often to the flat, even sleeping in the spare room when she felt like it, because neither of them was prepared to be bothered about what the neighbours might say. She persuaded him to have the lounge papered and she helped him choose a new lampshade and made him cushion covers for the settee. The house didn't yield up much in the way of information about him. There were one or two sentimental Edwardian pictures that had been his mother's favourites, of ringleted children with treacly eyes, but apart from that the ethos was male and minimal, that of a dry bachelor. The touches she brought were discreet, but they made a difference.

The only place she did not go was his bedroom. He did not keep the door closed. As she passed, she saw his British Homes Stores dressing-gown hung over a painted wooden chair, his brown leather slippers placed neatly awaiting his bare morning feet. A faded candlewick bedspread in what had once been a turquoise colour covered the high, old-fashioned iron and brass bedstead. There was a chest of drawers with a basin and ewer on it and two brass candlesticks, and not much else that she could see. Yet she did not go in until one day when he was doing something in the small garden attached to the flat and then she could not have identified what made her.

He wouldn't like it. Yet she realised as she stood by the bed that the room was helping her to know him. It was filled by a sense of desolation, and alone-ness, a faint masculine smell of tobacco, for he smoked lightly. And unexpectedly, the scent of lavender.

He never used after-shave. He was such a plain, dun-coloured man she was intrigued he should even have the scent of lavender in his room.

She stepped quickly over to the chest of drawers and pulled a drawer open. Shirts, socks, vests. All tidy. Underneath would be pullovers. She shouldn't be doing this, but she pulled another drawer open. It was filled with lace-edged panties. She quickly shut it again, but not before the scent of lavender came, strong and over-powering. And in some way she could not describe, male.

She stood uncertainly and then she became aware that he was behind her. She had not even heard him enter the flat, but he'd left his gardening shoes by the kitchen door.

She walked past him without saying anything and he followed her into the lounge. In a little her heart stopped its heavy pounding and settled into its regular beat. She picked up a cross-stitch sampler she was working on and inserted steady stitch after steady stitch.

"You were in my bedroom," he said.

"Yes."

"You've never been in my bedroom before."

"No."

"I don't mind you going," he said, steadily. "You can go in there whenever you like. I hope when we make it legal, eventually, you will feel you can go there whenever you like."

He looked at her in that guileless and honest way he did sometimes and she was the first to look away, for her mind was still swarming with questions she could not ask. Might never be able to ask.

"We are company for each other," he said, briefly, and then she heard him in the kitchen, washing his hands and then filling the kettle for a cup of tea.

That night she lay in the farm bed and heard the best bull in the county at his bellowing and for once did not read one of her romances in which the hero might say 'My darling one'.

She wondered if they would ever make it legal and could not look into the abyss if they did not.

9

Abercrombie and the Dodgy Situation

WHEN Farquharson wasn't painting, which was seldom, his whole physical being seemed to fall apart. Gaps appeared in the seams of his time-serving corduroys, fibrous holes in his jumpers and shirts; his hair stuck out like a cat's with the mange, he had intermittent toothache and his pale, reflective painter's eyes sank like drought-stricken lakes in the crumbling sand of his strafed and pulverised expression.

It was the desperate outward manifestation of his inward state, demonstrated now as he sat with the sole fruit of his loins, one Saffron, on Abercrombie's sofa, obsessively chewing a small hardened lump of cobalt blue on his mothy Zapata. The infant's face reflected his own, except that having no moustache to chew on, it wobbled its gums worriedly

166

over the boot of Paddington Bear on its towelling bib.

"She knows this guy is coming over from the States, and that I have to get the big pic to the gallery before the twenty-first," he keened. "You'd have thought she could put a few principles aside for once. But no. She insists it's my week for the Pureed Prune Princess here, that we entered the state of parenthood on the strict basis of shared responsibility. If you and Lulu could just keep an eye on her for a couple of days, I'd take her home at night. Since you're both on a week's leave . . . "

Abercrombie stared at his friend with all the unsullied enthusiasm of a cornered rat. He knew nothing of babies beyond the fact that you sometimes saw them on supermarket trolleys amidst the sugar and Surf and he felt Farquharson was trading on the fact that he and Lulu would soon have one of their own and that a little parental practice would not go amiss.

It was rotten, underhand and a presumption on friendship, a relationship Abercrombie was swiftly in the throes of redefining.

At the same time, he knew what Farquharson was up against in the frontierswoman attitude of Saffron's mother, Chris, determined as his own Lulu that the Red Indians of chauvinism should never have their scalps but that the covered waggons of the feminist movement should roll ever onwards towards the New Dawn in the West. Or something of that nature. It could be uncomfortable, making the trip with women such as these. You didn't get scorpions in your socks but you didn't get washed socks, either. Sometimes, half out of the waggon, you saw other men in houses with well scoured steps and almost surrendered to the waves of pinafored women in curlers at the windows. But you didn't get off. It got to be a way of life, like Sufism and beds of nails. It had its own exhilarations. Lulu never bored him. And Chris, though she chastened the life out of him, had found the secret of getting through the messy swamps of Farquharson's preoccupations and feeding him alternatives to perpetual pasta and mince.

"What's Chris doing?" he demanded.

"She's doing her shift at the Hostel for Traumatised Persons — "

"You mean Battered Wives?"

"No. They run it for both sexes now. Men get battered too," said Farquharson the painter, rubbing recent scar tissue caused by the end of a potato masher above his right eye.

Abercrombie sighed from the bottom of his wish to spend a few days writing the great definitive comic novel about television, with which he plastered over the sore bits of his psyche on days when everything went wrong at the Beeb studios.

So far, he had got little further than writing the (eventual) reviews in his head, with a wryly attentive one from Auberon Waugh, a heavy-footed one bringing in Wagner from Bernard Levin and one calling him a literary Fred Astaire from Benny Green.

But he had, after all, known Farquharson a long time, since they had both come to London, bound together by the provincial lad's dream of Making It, of treading all detractors, sniffy aunts and sarcastic teachers in the dust.

Even if they both now knew the truth — that London was a bad-tempered place inhabited by sharks and gulls, a desert outpost, a souk, a fools' bazaar — each in his way had found the True Capital City, among the mountains of the mind, that would never have been discoverable in Scotland. (For there the great Tsk-Tsk still lived behind the Terylene net, dragging the sad Beast of the Unconscious behind it, twitching obsessively at any departure from the laid-down-by-custom, burying all upstarts and innovators in the Kailyard muck.)

"OK." Abercrombie capitulated.

"Great! Great!" hooted Farquharson, and the baby, sensing parental relief, beamed like a Brussels financier who'd just put one over on the IMF.

"She eats anything," Farquharson reassured, unburdening a Habitat bag of tins of pureed fruit and veg, some dried milk and a feeding bottle.

"She won't need her nappy changed for a bit and if you put on Jagger singing *Jumping Jack Flash* you'll not have a peep out of her."

"Get back to your canvas," Abercrombie

snarled. He had no intention of changing the baby's nappy. He would wait till Lulu returned from her consciousness-raising cell. And once the painter had disappeared, he put Menuhin playing the Kreutzer on the record player, telling the infant severely it was better for the development of her soul.

She sat on the floor in a washed-out blue jumpsuit, flailing her arms good-naturedly and uttering sounds like 'Oomph' and 'Flump' with a sort of barmaid jollity. Wherever you touched her she seemed to be padded with nappies or clothes. Nervously Abercrombie picked her up after a bit. She buried a podgy fist in the flesh just under one eye and cried with vexation when he made her desist. He recited Stevie Smith's poem about the galloping cat to restore his own equilibrium, if not hers, though she displayed a modified pleasure as he imitated the cat's movements and wept stormily when he sat down from sheer exhaustion.

A quietish period followed, while he peered anxiously from the windows for a sight of his wife and the unequivocal aroma of rotten eggs indicated the urgency of changing the baby soon. Fortunately, Saffron did not seem to mind. She did her best to keep his mind on higher things with bedecked smiles and outbreaks of bubble-blowing. Abercrombie's mind began to fill with disturbed foreboding. What if Farquharson never came back? What if he and Chris were planning to flee the country? Supposing Lulu had gone into premature labour on the bus coming home and was at this very moment in a high bed with white sheets at Hammersmith Hospital? He recognised these for the sick fancies they were.

Nevertheless, he had started biting his nails for the first time in his life before Lulu's key turned in the front door lock. Her face brightened at the unexpected warmth of his greeting then changed to bafflement at the sight of Saffron chewing the *Radio Times*.

"How did she get here?"

"I sort of promised Farquharson we would look after her for the next day or two. He has a picture to finish — "

"You did *what*?" Even as she turned

172

a furious face towards him, Lulu was expertly bundling the baby into a clean nappy, jiggling her against her shoulder and soothing her with clucking mother-hen noises.

"Said we'd — well, more *you*, really — would sort of stand *in loco parentis*."

"I can't." Lulu was extremely positive. "I've a script to finish — "

"And you know I want to get down to The Novel."

"Bugger your novel."

"That's not very nice," said Abercrombie aggrievedly.

"What about Chris? *She's* the baby's mother — "

"She's being bolshie. Taking a stand. Says it's Farquharson's week for Fish Face there and that's all there is to it."

Lulu fed the infant in silence. Between swallowing spoonfuls of pureed prunes and custard, Saffron looked from one to the other with the none-too-hopeful stare of a prisoner at the bar, say one who had been caught shop-lifting with £400 in her purse.

Eventually, stuffed with food and milk, the baby inadvertently fell asleep.

Purposefully, Lulu got out her notes and began to write in her hasty, cramped scholar's hand at the table by the window. She had been researching for a programme on Borstals. Morosely, Abercrombie wondered why she never did any research into what husbands might like for their lunch, but then banished the thought as unworthy of the seventies in which he was privileged to be a male. He brought forth the spare, attenuated bones of his chef d'oeuvre, staring at the words as though they were in Swahili. He was as conscious of the baby as the Lilliputians must have been of Gulliver.

Two hours passed in muted breathing and laboured thought. Then there was a series of peremptory rings at the doorbell. Lulu shot to answer them like a small, round pellet and confronted the stone-faced, duffel-coated figure of Saffron's mother, Chris, BA (Notts). Behind her stood a pale-faced woman all in black, her face a mask for some Greek tragedy.

"Come in," said Lulu uncertainly, but the two women had already advanced well past the threshold. "This is Mrs

Karanopolous," Chris barked. "I've brought her here because if I leave her at the hostel he might come and attack her — "

"Who he?" asked Abercrombie. In a way it was pleasant to put The Novel to one side for a short while. He had just imagined what the Auberon Waugh review might be like if the latter had just had one of his little altercations with a member of the lumpen-proletariat.

"He her husband — I mean, he's her husband," said Chris.

"Ay-eeee," cried Mrs Karanopolous. "I get chance of good job at Marks and Sparks. He say no job. He say I stay in kitchen. He hit me here — and here." As she dramatically pulled up various parts of her clothing, Abercrombie looked delicately away. His mother, after all, had not allowed him to look at the combinations in the Co-op in case it was thought she went in for loose living.

"You see! Stereotypes again!" cried Chris. "Her husband thinks she should stay at home, even though her children are away all day at the comprehensive and she gets lonely as sin."

"Ay-eeee," agreed Mrs Karanopolous.

Chris looked down at the just-roused Saffron. "He told me he'd bring her here. I didn't think he'd have the nerve. After promising me motherhood wouldn't be smotherhood. The moment the going gets difficult, he caves in."

"But he has work to finish," protested Abercrombie.

"Yes, and if I give in this time, I've had it," vowed Chris vehemently. "I'll end up all bum and bosom like those poor sods down at the hostel. So blurred with bloody Valium they can't pick up a knife and fork and eat a decent meal. Living on tea and biccies. No thank you very much. I'd sooner go on the streets."

Abercrombie's mind had begun to wander profitlessly down one of its blind alleys — the speculation of how the earnest Chris might fare if she ever carried out her threat - when there was a noise outside the flat door not unlike the bombardment of Stalingrad. Above thumps and bangs could be heard an excitable male voice uttering Mediterranean oaths and another with a laconic Strathclyde resonance urging him to cool it.

Bravely, as Abercrombie acknowledged, in view of his own boneless knees, Lulu threw open the flat door. A chunky man with a swarthy complexion, eyes flashing knives, all but fell into the hall, with Farquharson not inches behind him. Just then, as though on cue, Saffron let out a blood-curdling screech that would not have disgraced the participants of Wounded Knee.

"Where is my Arianna?" demanded Mr Karanopolous, for it was he.

"He's going to murder her," Farquharson affirmed. "Seems he followed her and Chris here. When I arrived he was arguing with the porter."

Chris planted her scrawny bejeaned figure squarely in front of her protegée. "He'll have to murder me first."

"Wha-at?" bellowed Karanopolous.

"Listen," said Farquharson slowly. He planted a paint-splattered hand on the other man's shoulder. "You hurt this wee person here and I'll personally mince you into pussy pieces and feed you to the cat. Do you get my meaning, Jimmy?"

Karanopolous pulled his arms back into their sleeves and his neck back into its socket. His eyes were still bulging dangerously.

"This — " indicating Chris — "is your *wife*?"

"Never you mind what our relationship is," said Farquharson. He looked at Chris and said almost kindly, "You should remember — you're no' very big."

"You big ape! You great, unfeeling, gormless, selfish beast!" Chris raged. She catapulted herself towards him and began kicking furiously at his shins. "You got me into this. If you'd keep your promises — "

Mrs Karanopolous, whose face had been registering every expression from outrage to bewilderment, suddenly interposed her person between Farquharson and Chris. To Chris she said, "He is bad to you? Then I will fight him as you fight for me." And she brought a heavy black handbag across the painter's back with a thud like a hundredweight of coal being dropped down a basement. Farquharson fell to his knees.

"Keys! Pax! Whatever the Greek

equivalent of hands-off is," he pleaded. He held out his hands to the others in an effective gesture of supplication. "I only came here to take the baby back. As I was painting I thought to myself: I'm a selfish, no-good bastard. Abercrombie no more wanted to have Saffron than Ted Heath wants to be best friends with Margaret Thatcher."

A small snort that might have been a denial issued from somewhere between Abercrombie's nose and throat. He looked like a guilty gnu.

Chris's arms fell to her sides. "Did you really think that?" she demanded. "But what about your painting? I suppose just this once I could have made an exception — "

"Woman!" Karanopolous thundered at his wife. "Why you hit this man? You hit someone, you hit me."

"I keel you," spat Mrs Karanopolous. "I spit on you. I never come back!"

"WHEESHT!"

The magisterial command had come from Abercrombie. "I suggest we all sit down and have a calming drink. All this noise is bad for the baby." He looked at Lulu, who had Saffron on her lap. The effect might have been disarming, except that because of Lulu's bump there was very little lap left. Saffron squirmed and cried.

Mrs Karanopolous advanced and took the baby in her arms. Immediately Saffron stopped crying. There was something immensely right about the comfortable black-clad matron and the way she held and handled the obstreperous child. "Iss all right," she murmured. "Arianna is here." Saffron uttered a loud burp and gave a sheepish smile.

* * *

"It is a compromise, of course," said Lulu sternly.

"If it works, does it matter?" demanded Abercrombie. His week's leave had gone in and he had succeeded in writing only half a paragraph of The Novel. It did not seem to matter. Lulu had finished *her* work and in her unpredictable way had just provided him with a meal fit for the gods — chicken laved in lemon sauce and a toffee-topped apple pie to which he was particularly partial.

"Arianna minds the baby while Farquharson finishes the painting," said Lulu. "Chris does her thing at the hostel. Karanopolous raises no objections to his wife helping out, because he says looking after children isn't work. Compromise, all the way."

"Look," said Abercrombie. "I might as well finish this apple thing, mightn't I?" He could see his wife was gathering her hortatory cudgels, but he sank into the pleasant mental terrain where once again he could watch The Novel hover on the creative horizon, like a shimmer of heat in the desert. Compromise he knew all about, but toffee-apple pie did tend to rot a man's moral fibre.

10

Something Sportive

"ARE you happy?" he would say to her and she would answer, smiling up at him, because he was good-looking, so much handsomer than she could ever have hoped for, "Yes, of course I am." But five years after the marriage, her first, his second, it wasn't necessarily so. She was beginning to feel hemmed in by the restraints he placed upon her and she saw she wasn't her own woman any more, but his Galatea, the one who wouldn't get away, as his first had done.

He'd picked her young and he'd picked her — well, nicely ordinary, seeing her making out smudged and cryptic receipts in her uncle's yard in the village and knowing nothing of the books she read, in the long slow afternoons when nobody came, or the dreams she dreamed in her lethargic cocoon.

She had wanted him, because young though she was she had felt sorry for him, had wanted to mother him, to make it better for him. Her yearning had gone out like a silken thread, drawing him to her. She had always mothered kittens, puppies, her sister's children, she was an overwhelmingly kind child in those days, as though by being maternal she could bind up some of her own hurts and deficiencies, and these were many. No one had ever said she had any looks, or any brains, or any place in the scheme of things. She had been the messenger, the servant, the stop-gap, the butt, the youngest, the meek little item with nothing very engaging about her at all, and not even enough spirit to stand up for herself.

If she'd had that, she would have gone to college, and not let her lackadaisical parents go on drinking, smoking and frittering the money that should have gone into her and her sister's education and into decent clothes that would have helped them to feel somebody.

So when he asked her if she was happy, she always said yes, and she did her best to be a good wife to him and mother to the son and daughter who were in his custody. She had done so much better for herself than anyone could have expected. She had a lovely home, fitted with all the latest gadgets and there was even a swimming-pool in the back garden. Her sisters were distinctly jealous of her, wondering how she'd done it, being so ordinary and nondescript, whereas they had pretty, cloudy hair and long legs and yet their men had grimy finger-nails, stubby figures and no conversation worth mentioning. He was a computer expert and had kept the desirable house from his first, disastrous, marriage. It stood right on the edge of the village, with views of half of Middle England all around it and a landscape painted with corn and rape in the spring and golden semi-circles of forest in the autumn. You had the feeling, living in the house, that you were part of nature and history, even though it stood where on a good day you could see the conurbation that was grimy Manchester. She liked to see the distant mill chimneys, to think of the chapmen climbing over the Pennines with their silk buttons, to imagine the rough hill roads resounding to coaches and highwaymen. She liked to feel she was where she was, right in the middle of the county and the country where she had been born, as much a part of it all as the flowers that bloomed by the wayside and, in the spring, down in the mysterious woods. She was a poet in spirit, though she did not know it. But of course there was so much she did not know about herself. It was only just beginning, this particular vein of information and it had begun with him asking her if she was happy and her realising that definition had not been given to her. Not yet. It was still to come.

She had gone through the initiation of acquitting herself, she thought, reasonably well. She had learned to cook and be an economical housewife. By trial and error she had developed a style of dressing that was stylish without being flamboyant. He never complained about what she spent on clothes; in fact, he quite enjoyed going with her to boutiques and department stores and urging her to be adventurous. In the same way, a good hairdresser had tamed the thick and unruly pale brown hair into a shoulder-length style and blonde highlights gave a gamine charm to her narrow, foxy features. One thing the observant onlooker might have noticed was that she still walked in a stilted, unsure manner, haltingly, like a small animal crossing a twilight road, and that she did not keep her shoulders back, but hunched them, almost as though she expected blows. But since she was not aware she did this, she could not do anything about it.

Was she happy in bed with him? Reasonably so. Her kindness made this possible. Was she in harmony with his children? Again there was little cause for complaint. Since she was not a positive creature and did not impose any fierce constraints upon them, they jogged along without too much unexpected turmoil.

The basis of their life together was her gratitude. That, and the fury and resentment he felt at his first wife's abandonment of him, which for the obvious reason of self-respect he kept well hidden. He knew he was above average in intelligence, even in looks and certainly in sexual performance so why, therefore, had it happened? And how could he make sure it would never happen again:- By locking her into his way of thinking and doing things and not allowing her even to think of having a job, which in the beginning was quite in accord with her timidity but which might have appealed as she grew older, sharper and in her new milieu, a bit more sophisticated and woman-of-the-worldly.

And, of course, by sharing interests. As she had not had a chance to develop any, marrying so young, these were mainly his — vintage cars, crosswords, wine-making and morris dancing. It wasn't very strict morris dancing. It was mixed with floral and country and had women in it, because you couldn't always get enough men.

People were always amused when he owned to the latter and he could not have quite explained it except that it was a bit like choosing the last house on the outskirts of the village, an alliance he kept with his childhood love of things country. Something in him responded to the bell-hung vernal costumes, the simple music, the satisfying predictability of the dance patterns, the banging of staffs and the clatter of clogs. It was a rare juxtaposition to his cerebral working-life, it took him back to earlier simplicities like the smell of grass and animals and the sunshine yellow of buttercups and yes, some part of him was pleased if friends were surprised by the incongruity of it, the change from neat-bearded, sober-suited analyst to country satyr with flowers in his hat and ruffs to his shirt. He enjoyed being something of a conundrum.

At first she resisted. She had been to pop concerts with her sisters and school friends, she listened when he was out to rock tapes and heavy metal. The simple pinafores and embroidered blouses, the floral wreaths and white stockings which the women wore reduced her to hysterics. But as usual he had his way. She picked up the rhythms of the dances without trouble and was soon being congratulated by the other dancers as a natural. She even enjoyed it. She caught the scent of something sportive and primeval and her head was up, like a young doe's. She began to look forward to the fêtes and fayres and country markets where they performed, when the weather permitted, for charity.

He did not care much for the way in which their leader, the man they called the Old Goat, because of a certain lascivious glint in his eye, fastened on to her as the star, insisting she led off the sets with him, or took the last bow. He himself was often teamed with a stout, breathless forty-year-old who turned an alarming shade of beetroot as the dancing went on. What started off as natural pride in his wife's prowess soured into a mean-spirited challenge that she was in danger of making a fool of herself.

"What do you mean?" she demanded.

"You're supposed to fit into the dance. It's the overall effect that matters. But *you* have to dig your heels in that bit harder. And the way you toss your head, you'd think you were Makarova. The others don't like it."

"They haven't said anything. They would say if they didn't like it. I just enjoy myself. What's wrong with that?"

"It isn't *Opportunity Knocks*. You're not auditioning for the Palace Theatre.

What we have here is an old tradition, country folk enjoying a country way of life. No one person is supposed to stand out from the rest."

"Can I help it if I'm a natural?" She had cooked the evening meal after a day out at a country fair and he had noticed how after these events her domestic performance left much to be desired. The potatoes were over-cooked and she served the broad beans in a slapdash manner, with steak that had passed that vital stage where the juices ran to the fork, and then had the nerve to follow up with a shop-bought apple pie and something she said defiantly was a cream substitute but just as good as.

He could feel irritation curdle in him, with the need to make her toe the line, keep up her standards. Look at the life he had given her! She had come to him with two faded dresses to her back and an old shop overall.

"Just don't get above yourself, dear." His two children, in the manner of modern youngsters enjoying the ersatz, junk-food cream and the needle-match between the adults, narrowed their eyes as they watched first one, then the other.

This time she did not back down. She met his gaze with defensive hostility in her own, her silence burning him up more effectively than any words. It could be said that that was the evening that battle was joined, except that battle was not quite the correct word for it. She had broken away from his dominance, rather, and was defining what happiness was in her own way. She still loved him and avoided argument with him, but when he had to go abroad on business, she fed the collusive children and herself on junk food, played old Bob Marley records and danced about the living-room, barefoot, when the Communards or Shaking Stevens were on television. She went to dance and aerobic classes and became conscious of her young, lithe figure in a way she never had before, lavishing creams and lotions on it after her bath or shower, shaving and smoothing her legs, painting toe as well as finger-nails. Sometimes she wondered if all this had something to do with him not wanting any further children. It was as though she babied her own body by way of retaliation or to fend off more basic demands.

He had taken to brass-rubbings, looking at old country churches, taking his son with him to improve the boy's sense of history. He said he might go off the whole idea of morris dancing, but she threw all his old persuadings back at him. The exercise was good for him, his life was too sedentary, it was either dancing or golf and he hated the latter, he knew he did.

And the old pastime still held some allure on a bright day, the sun glinting through the summer trees, people and their dogs sauntering through tents and marquees filled with crafts, jams, and flowers, the kestrel-handlers putting their feathery proteges through their test-flights, children staring owl-eyed at the sheep, the Clydesdale horses, the niffy cows, penned for their inspection and instruction, the ice-cream van dispensing cornets, the hazy smoke from hamburger barbecues and then the accordion music, the tambourines, the jangle of bells that signified the start of the morris dancing, the May games that had begun with

Robin Hood and Maid Marian, back in the mists and myths and legends of Merrie England. The perfect antidote to too much world travel, to too much computerese, to motorways, and balance-sheets and telephones and all else.

Perhaps it was just that he was growing older. He had always prided himself on his physical fitness, he did press-ups each day and rode an exercise bicycle. He got out of breath more easily, nonetheless, and his calves ached. He found it harder to remember the routines of some of the dances and earned clucking remonstrances from his female partners. It seemed to him that the harder he pushed himself, the easier it got for her. She danced like the personification of the May spirit itself, her slim body so spritely and responsive, her foxy face animated and pretty in a way it wasn't normally.

His work was growing more demanding. He was in line for a directorship and that would mean more home entertaining. She would have plenty of responsibility then, so perhaps she would drop her increasing references to either (a) starting a baby or (b) getting a job.

"I don't think I could face another mewling infant," he told her honestly. "I've been through the parenthood bit, the getting up in the night. I need all my concentration at the moment for The Business." He always capitalised his work in his own mind. It was the one area in his life where he had been consistently successful and to feed the feeling of gratification it gave him he was prepared to sacrifice a great deal. He needed her to support him. He made no denial of that. She must see how important she was to him. This was a fairly successful line to take with her: the maternal in her responded. But at the same time she saw her life flowing away from her, her stepchildren growing up and the possibility of a child of her own remaining a will o' the wisp, like the prospects of a job or even a little business of her own.

Friends took a more independent line. They joked that she might never have heard of women's lib. They went out and took what they wanted from life, fed their husbands on convenience foods, went to college. But they had not had her uncertain start and they did not have her sense of gratitude. She did her best to balance the past with the present, to weigh the undoubted benefits of her life with him against the increasingly vague and unnamed dissatisfactions. So when they had one of their intense bouts of lovemaking they tended to do this rather than make love on a regular basis — and he asked her if she was happy she would not often say directly, as in the old days 'Yes, of course I am', but 'What do you think?' or 'I suppose so' and allow herself to look a little wistful.

That summer, the morris dancers were in demand.

"I can't keep up with it," he acknowledged and took it for granted she would not go if he did not. They had endless tussles of will over this.

The Old Goat, who was responsible for putting on the displays, rang up and made it clear that he would feel terribly let down if she at least did not put in an appearance.

"Well, go then," he said gracelessly.

"I'd rather you came too."

"Just as of now I have better things to

do. Namely, work." Travelling, hot dusty airports, too many late-night whiskies to buck him up, were making him short-tempered.

The Old Goat, whom she naturally did not call by that name, but rather Joe, was delighted to have her as his sole partner for a while. Nobody could lead off a dance with such style, such brio as these two. His dark Priapic eyes twinkled at her above his roguish beard. Together, somebody said, they were the very embodiment of the old May games, the Abbot of Unreason and his Queen of the May. Their performance pulled up everybody else in the troupe: the musicians had never played so merrily or well, the busty young matrons and younger girls with their partners, even the callow lads drawn into it all half against their will, had never romped through the dancing in quite such a spirit of fun, abandonment and commitment.

She was always buoyed up after these outings, by the praise, the easy company, the simple, open-air food afterwards, above all by the open admiration in Joe's eyes.

"Watch out," the other women warned her, laughing. "He'll try it on, you know." Of course, you acknowledged it was there, the frisson of desire, the sexual undercurrents, the press on the fingers, the meaningful gaze. The whole thing was a celebration, a fertility rite, even if a mickey-taking twentieth-century element had crept in.

But she did not intend to let it get out of hand. She saw herself as being in love with her husband. If he was moody and tired sometimes, she put that down to the natural progression of time, and the strains of a demanding job. He still brought her chocolates and perfume and praised her when people came to dinner. Sometimes she thought she was a kind of status symbol, like his Filofax and his smart BMW and that this was why he wanted people to see her as smarter, wittier, more competent that she really was. But other people, their friends, also got by on half-truths, evasions, pretences, romancing. Why couldn't they all stop this silly game of Better Thy Neighbour? Sometimes it was as though a great, uncomfortable wedge was lodged between herself and her husband and she was forever trying to shift it, get through to him, make him take her for what she was and what she had been.

When he was away, she did think sometimes of Joe, and his beady, speculative, naughty eye. What would it be like, knowing him better? Much about him was vague. He ran a vague sort of printing or publishing business. He was vaguely interested in photography, painting, alternative healing. He had vaguely been married and was vaguely no longer so. He had a vague daughter in Australia. He loved women: talking to them, dancing with them, flirting with them. At least two of the women in the troupe had had affairs with him. This was why the other girls warned her to be careful of him. They did it half-seriously, not really condemning him. He was just Joe. He tried it on. At the moment, he was trying it on with her and the knowledge made her smile, somewhere deep inside her where may things grew, primroses and buttercups and all things bright. But she was a happily married

198

woman and that was that.

When her husband became moodier, even, she thought, to the point of depression, she wondered if it was her own dereliction that had caused it. They had been married for quite a long time, after all, and had reached the stage where they picked up things unsaid, feelings that were never articulated. Was her own vague dissatisfaction communicating itself to him? Where she grew restless and a little wild and argumentative when she felt unfulfilled, he went into one of his brown studies. That was what his mother had called them and it was now the family name.

"What's up?" She had cooked him fillet de boeuf en croute, sieved the carrots with cream and nutmeg, made a stomach-soothing creme brulee with raspberries underneath, all to no avail. (They had not been to bed together for six weeks. He slept with his face away from her, curled in the foetal position.)

"Nothing."

"Something is. Your face would curdle cream."

Later, he told her. The children had

gone to a movie and he lay with his head in her lap. She thought she saw tears in his eyes.

"Alana. When I was in London," he said, "I saw her coming out of the Army and Navy in Victoria Street." She was wearing a beige suit with a navy blouse." He was talking about his first wife. It was the first she'd heard of it.

"When was this?"

"About two months ago."

"Why didn't you tell me?"

"For precisely the reason you demonstrate. I thought it would upset you."

"But it's you that is upset. She still has an emotional hold on you." She said with a tragic clarity and resignation, "You still love her."

"No." He sat up now and held her close. "Far from loving her, I hate her. For what she did to me and the kids."

"Did you speak to her?" she asked, remorselessly.

"I have nothing to say to her. Now or ever."

"But *then* — that day — did you speak to her?"

"Of course not. What do you take me for?"

"Did she see you?"

"I think she might have done."

She returned his embrace then. "Well, it was something and nothing, wasn't it?"

He wanted to pour out what he felt to her, all of it, the dreadful pain of lost love, the leap of the heart he'd experienced on seeing his first wife, her lovely absorbed face, the way she dressed now, the essence of fragile chic. Like a will o' the wisp, her memory taunted him daily, so that he found himself caught up in useless fantasies of getting her back. But how could he say any of this to the loyal and loving girl who was his second wife, who had tried so hard to please him? He loved her too. The sensible, everyday, pragmatic part of him loved her, but something he could not tame, could not analyse, could not eradicate, broke away from reality and insisted on being with his first wife."

His agony broke out now in a muffled cry and she held him, his face turned into her shoulder and said, "It will be better now you have told me."

He looked at her and said, with all his heart, "You are so much better a person than she is. You are good and true and kind where she is shallow, cold and selfish. I suppose I was knocked back because I hadn't seen her since she bolted."

"Put it behind you," she said, soothingly. "Now that we've talked about it, things will be better. You'll see."

"I'll try to get home early tomorrow night," he promised her. "We'll go out for a meal. Just the two of us." Then they went up to bed and they made love, for the first time in six weeks. He went up the stairs slowly, like a man with a burden and she walked behind, her head bowed, her mind unable to recall the face of the woman who had gone before her, though he could remember every line and every movement of mood, every turn of the head.

★ ★ ★

"Come to the fête," she invited him. "You haven't danced for so long." She gazed through the window. "And it's a golden sort of day. Just look at it."

He shrugged on a pullover and joined her by the window. From the house on the far edge of the village you could see Middle England in May. Trees that had burst the bonds of close buds and were shaking out their green glory; blossom so prodigal the eye resisted so much pink. Fields, turning subtly, slowly from dark winter green to emerald, to gold and every shade and shadow in between.

In the country lane leading past their house, two little girls stopped under a cherry tree and shook its silky trunk, so that pale pink petals showered on their heads like confetti and they danced like fauns. In a field nearby, a ewe peremptorily ordered its lamb to return to her side. It did so kicking up elegant spindly legs. "Everything dances," she said. "Come to the morris dancing with me today."

"No," he said. "You know I can't. You know how much work I have in hand." He said it reluctantly, for the spring did lay its hold on him and when she had gone he left his work undone for as long as he dared, and from his study window counted the trees he knew in his garden. Poplar, oak, beech. Sycamore, hawthorn, elm. Lilac, laburnum, acer. Shimmering birch. Big spreading chestnut. He went down and made himself a rallying cup of coffee, feeling a certain freedom at being on his own. But I don't want *you*, he told the will o' the wisp who ran ahead, who turned a bright head at corners. I will make you fade, eventually, by the strength of my will, and I will love my other wife, my second wife, as she deserves.

The second wife made her way through the scattered crowds at the fête, her white broderie anglaise petticoat rustling with starch, the ribbons from the garland on her blonde head streaming gaily behind her. She could hear the sounds of concertina and flute and a clatter of clogs as the children of some of the dancers, dressed to ape their parents, practised for the day when they too would perform these strange, jolly rituals from the heart of the greenwood and meadow.

The Old Goat smiled at her, the girls greeted her, patting her arms, adjusting the flowers in her hair and the young men gave her shy, sidelong looks.

Just recently, like a thin, piercing knife, she had felt a kind of metaphysical pain somewhere near where she imagined her heart to be. She knew what it was. She had known at the start of the marriage that the knife might well go deeper with the years.

But it was a magical day. The sun glittered, everything was new and innocent and fresh and you could not help but be a part of it. The second wife danced out her sorrows and her tribulations and knew what it was again to be part of the May, young and vibrant and with the sap running wild.

"You've never danced better," said Joe and his dark eyes gleamed like the brook and glittered like the buttercups with appreciation. "How about coming over after this and I'll show you the photos I took last time?"

His hand held hers so firmly and was never damp, like that of the callow boys, but always guiding, leading, claiming.

"I might, Joe," she said, and shivered like an aspen, knowing it to be true. "I just might."

11

Going To See Pavlova

"BEAT your arms. Up and down," said my father. "Now more gently. Your arms are the swan's wings. She is getting weaker and weaker. Her neck droops. The strength is ebbing from her body. She is dying. She folds her wings to her body. Her head sinks into her downy feathers. She is dead."

My sister and I put all the feeling we were capable of into interpreting our father's version of the Dying Swan. He had seen Pavlova once and never forgotten it. He wanted us to know how wonderful it had been. Meg was better at it than me. She could do good arms and was younger and slighter. My knees were battle-scarred and purple from washing them in cold water and I wasn't built to be Pavlova, but I felt the part, oh, how I felt it. Freezing pond, failing strength, the poor wings getting slower and slower.

During the cold winter months in the country we got a big coal fire going and lived our alternative lives. If it wasn't Pavlova, it could be Sarah Bernhardt. My father had seen her, too. Yes, just the once, after she'd had her leg off. How marvellous she had been! 'To be or not to be,' he recited, 'that is the question.' We saw nothing amiss in a nine-year-old playing a one-legged old woman playing the Prince of Denmark. My brother was talked into leaving his cigarette cards alone for a while to be master of ceremonies. Meg and I would dress up in lace curtains and old sheets, out in the lobby. Then Billy would announce "Ladeez and gentlemen, you are going to see Pavlova dance the Dying Swan, followed by Miss Sarah Bernhardt doin' Hamlet," and the lobby door would open dramatically and tripping over our sheets the troupe of two would pour in, eyes glazed, cheeks red, heads full of the theatrical images our father had conjured up for us.

My mother was remarkably tolerant of these histrionics. She would sit doing her immaculate necessary darnings of jumper elbows or sock heels, hissing with disappointment when her wool ran out, or her soft hazel eyes would gaze into the coal flames while her toes toasted on the fender.

The next morning we would go off to school and my father would try to earn a bob or two. In the big cardboard suitcase there would be packets of margarine and tea and he would climb the stairs of tenements and sell them to women in print overalls with tight permed hair or marcel waves. Well, sometimes he would sell them. It was the thirties and there were soup kitchens. The women were as hard up as we were. My mother said my father could charm the birds out of the trees but once purses were emptied of their coppers, that was that. My father gave tick but it was a bad idea. He never got back the money he was owed.

"*C'est la vie*," said my father. He had picked up the lingo in France during the war. That's where he'd seen the dead horses and that's where he'd lain out in No Man's Land for two nights and days, breathing in the mustard gas that had gone for his lungs.

208

"That damned war," said my mother. "He was the finest dancer you ever saw, before that damned war. He had two shops and a thousand pounds in the bank." Clearly, it had not been a good idea to volunteer. "If there's another, I'll do it all over again," said my father defiantly. "We couldn't depend on the Frogs."

"I don't know where the next penny is coming from," said my mother.

"The Lord will provide," said my father, looking scrupulously round the house to see what could next be popped at Uncle's. My mother stored the pawn-tickets in the teapot of her wedding china. Soon you had to press down quite hard to get the lid to go on.

"The two finest sights in the world," said my father, "are a beautiful woman and a beautiful racehorse." My mother gave him an old-fashioned look. He was going to the races, to make a book. He had a good head for figures, a big leather bag, a folding stool to stand on and a big band going across his chest with his name on it. I polished his boots and my mother brushed his bowler. He looked sharp, dapper. His clerk was the friendliest, most affable little man alive, one Jazz O'Neill. They were a great combination. Sometimes.

Saturday night. My mother sat with her hat on, two spots of rouge on her cheeks. My brother hoped for the 'Autocar' and my sister and I for the 'Sunbeam' so we could read about Daisy Bell in Sherwood Forest. But it all depended on how these undependable creatures with unlikely names like Dusty Miller and Fogarty's Fancy had performed on the track, whether the going had been soft or hard, the jockeys on their form or off it.

We watched him coming up the dusty country track. Lean as a blade. Puffing those damaged lungs. Sometimes he pretended to have lost when he hadn't. On good nights the silver half-crowns and florins spilled across the table, the pound and ten shilling notes appeared from pockets like magic. Mother returned from shopping with a box of cakes tied up with purple ribbon, with chocolate liqueurs and the longed-for periodicals, the latest PG Wodehouse from the Boots

Library for father, sometimes even a new hat for herself which always seemed to cost 4s 11d.

"Don't go near him," said my mother on Remembrance Day. My father disappeared into the Front Room and stayed there for half an hour. "That bloody war," she would add. "And he's too proud even to take a pension."

She had her own memories. Of Belgian refugees pouring into the fever hospital where she nursed. "Tell us about little Mons," we would plead. Mons was a tiny Belgian girl, named after the battle where the soldiers thought they had seen angels in the sky. Covered with tubercular sores, she had been in frequent trouble with Sister for wetting or dirtying the bed.

She called my gentle dark-haired mother Mama and would call out defiantly. "I shit the bed again, Mama. My mother would clean her up, wrap her in a blanket and sing to her in front of the ward fire. "Poor little thing," she would reflect to us, "she was in agony most of the time." And of course she died. We always wished the ending could be different.

In our small garden, we could at least grow some of our own vegetables. The pet rabbit ate the lettuce and worse, those of our neighbours as well. I was a good brambler. My mother made pounds of jam and jelly, and big satisfying soda scones with milk from the sour-milk cart. Then as gambling fever took ever-tightening hold on my father, and local bets were placed when it was too cold for visits to the racecourse, there were arguments about money.

"I never thought my life would be like this," said my mother. My father asked her if she remembered his taking her to *The Maid of the Mountains* and sang her 'After the Ball'. We waited to see if she would forgive him but as the holes got bigger in our shoes it got harder.

The next thing we were taught was Rabbie. Burns. 'To a Mouse', 'To a Mountain Daisy', 'To Mary in heaven', 'To a Louse, on seeing one on a lady's bonnet at Church'. I plucked at the heartstrings with a touch of the Bernhardt, my sister made 'em laugh. We were entered for the competitions run by the schools. Got up in our best skirts and jumpers, hair ribbons carefully ironed, we would set out on the long, dark country walk to the bus stop, our mother warning us to keep out of the puddles.

Inhaling the aromatic smoke from his Potter's Asthma Cure, my father and a lofty Billy stayed at home with the cat, listening to Radio Athlone or Harry Roy on the battery wireless.

Pointing out the North Star as we set out, he apologised for not having the puff to join us. "But that is your star and it will watch over you." It did, too. We came home prize-laden and triumphant, our feet crackling the ice on the now-frozen puddles, joyously greeting the kettle steaming on the range and the hot toast crisping at the edges on the trivet. There was even a gold medal that inevitably got pawned — and retrieved, and pawned, and retrieved, and pawned, till finally swallowed up in Uncle's jackdaw recesses of lost domestic treasures.

"The quality of mercy is not strained," said my father. "It droppeth as the gentle rain from heaven upon the earth beneath." My mother pulled the hooked rag rug from under his feet and took it out into the garden to beat it with the carpet-beater. Hard. On Mondays she filled the house with airing washing. Bloomers festooned the pulley. She put down newspapers on the clean lino for us to walk on and there was the dreaded porridge for tea. "Some men won't shift their arses," she said, pointedly, having learned to curse while nursing. In the dead of winter my father got a job digging 'founds' — I presume, road foundations.

My mother saw him and wept. "It was not for your father," she said. "Not that job. Better the tea and margarine yet." He worked in a grocer's shop and for three weeks bounty ruled. My mother bloomed under the security of thirty shillings a week. But my father could not stand not to be his own man. He and my uncle, that dead ringer for Mr Micawber, discussed growing mushrooms. The only snag was, they did not have a cellar.

Feeling better, my father decreed we should see a pantomime. The greatest Glasgow droll of all, Tommy Loren. For some reason I cannot recall, possibly economic, only I went with him. We climbed laboriously up into the sixpenny gods, vertiginous and breathless. There was a running joke about Mrs Broon's wee pie shop. I could not hear very well what was going on. "The best of the music-hall is passing away," said my father, blaming it on the pictures, which he regarded as cheap and meretricious. "But you have seen the best."

We were leaving the house in the country behind us.

No more early Sunday morning walks, when he'd let us take off our socks and shoes and paddle in the burn. No more sightings of our mother at the door of our cottage, waving us down for breakfast, spiced ham and eggs for the adults if 'the doggies', the local greyhounds, had obliged. No more guising at Hallowe'en, no more rushing through the dark in the game of Fiery Cross. The war was coming. We could hear the rat-tat-tat of the guns at practice on the rifle range not far away. My father still had his pocket book with instructions on setting up his machine gun in the Great War and his diary with all those references to the stench of dead horses. "If I could, I'd go again," he fretted, and meant it. My mother sighed.

My father did not have much longer to live. "That bloody war," said my mother, meaning that there had only been one war, one Great War, not the farcical pretence of a war that the second one was in the initial stages.

I thought I was going to be a writer.

"'This above all,' said my father, "'to thine own self be true, And it must follow as the night the day, Thou cans't not then be false to any man'."

The blue eyes blazed. The body was skeletal. He read his Shakespeare and Wodehouse and sang the songs from the shows he'd taken my mother to, when he had still been the best dancer in the hall.

We had to borrow to bury him. There was no stone above his grave, only a young tree from the garden. Better than any stone, said my mother, and she was right. He'd known every tree by name.

Poverty is only in the mind, he would say. Use your imagination.

Well, I can. I do. I've always been

able to picture Pavlova. If it all gets a bit mixed up with scabby knees and big coal fires tonguing up the chimney, that isn't my father's fault. Who is to say it's any the worse for that, anyway?

12

Over The Hill

THE car bought from Father's legacy was neat and bright and new, in the soft, pale leafy green that was fashionable that spring and it was somehow incongruous to be decanting the three old women into it for the after-lunch drive into the Peaks.

Not that Matron hadn't turned them out a treat, Joanna thought. Their hair had been newly washed and set, they wore their best coats and their cheeriest smiles, but of course, they creaked and hobbled and stumbled and in the case of the oldest of all, Ernestine, had to be held up and practically frog-marched, for her poor old feet had almost forgotten how to walk, how to put one in front of the other. Joanna began to wonder at the wisdom of the outing, three geriatrics in her total care, but for goodness sake, if you didn't allow the altruistic impulse to flower once in a while, what hope was there for the world? And as her friend Elizabeth Carter the headmistress said, they still had their health and strength and could go on cruises when they felt like it, so it behoved them to help the older generation, and in Joanna's case, it passed the time and kept her from missing Father.

Florence sat in the front. She had never lost her confidence that life owed her a good time and could still manage a bit of banter. She wore vivid green and her lipstick was authentic 1940 Joan Crawford red.

When the gardener at Pentagon Chase, that desirable Rest Home for the Elderly, advised her to be good if she could not be careful, she remembered the reply with ease: chance would be a fine thing. She was saucy but remembering her claim to refinement in front of lippy upstart workmen, of whom George, the gardener, at sixty, was one. She was also a shade — just a shade — rebuking. Florence had once been formidable.

Una wasn't sure where they were going. She allowed herself to be shoved and manoeuvred into the back seat of the dainty little car and once there, her rickety frame settled comfortably into the knubbly tweed, the late morning sun surging warmly through the sparkling clean windows, she knew something pleasant was afoot. In the circumstances, when voices were light and bright, even if you did not hear them all that clearly, and faces filled with goodwill, you smiled and smiled like anything. That reassured everybody. Una's teeth clicked up and down with the effort as she perceived a distant need to go to the bathroom. She hoped fervently she would not leak, not in the pretty new green car, but she couldn't face the travail of getting out and getting back in again, so she sat still and hoped the faint tickle in her bladder would go away.

Ernestine was aware when the jogging and jarring stopped. Some time soon it would all have to stop. A lot of it already had. The strength wasn't there, to respond. But somebody *had* said tea. She still liked eating. Eating still felt like it always did, in fact, better than ever. Especially cake. And somebody had said tea. Ernestine clung to that, doggedly, as Matron and Joanna practically lifted her along the path to the car, her little stick-like legs and feet in the big brown shoes getting the message to move just a little too late to be relevant. In the car she wondered briefly what the weight was on her shoulders, a terrible weight. It was her grey checked coat. Then she did not think of anything at all.

"Here we are then, all merry and bright," said Joanna, taking her place in the driver's seat and adjusting her seat-belt. Matron, big-bummed and preoccupied, had already disappeared through the front doors of Pentagon Chase, with its gleaming brass carriage lamps and reassuring tubbed flowers. (As to why matrons were always big-bummed, Joanna had no answer. Maybe all the tea they drank filtered into the tissues.)

"Where are we going?" asked Florence.

"A mystery tour," Joanna responded. "Over the hills and far away. Are we all settled?" She let in the clutch and the car bowled down the hilly street, the laburnum and lilac still dripping from the morning's heavy rain but everything beginning to burnish and shine as a hot, improvident sun imposed itself on the Cheshire day.

"We are going to be lucky!" Joanna carolled. "Spring has finally sprung." It had in fact been a sulky, dragging-its-feet kind of May, cloudy, chilly, reluctant, but it had given the countryside time to shake out its new clothes and now everything seemed to have reached perfect pitch for the ladies' afternoon out. The may trees primped in their pink abundance, the leggy birch shook their delicate leaves around them like so many lacy shawls and heavy, green and priapic the beech and oak and sycamore hid secrets in their depths.

"There are lambs everywhere," Florence observed incontrovertibly. Ten minutes later, Una said "Lambs," pointing them out excitedly. The car left the Dark Peak behind them and climbed into roaring sunshine. Drystone dykes washed as clean as a Monday blackboard intersected fields infested with cattle and sheep. In the little towns and hamlets they passed through, people were out painting shop fronts and cutting grass verges, pulling out spent daffodils and putting in petunias.

It was such a nice day, so full of the bounce and vigour and promise of the young year, that Joanna felt full of the love and generosity that comes when an impulse for good sees itself fulfilled. There is perhaps no tonic quite so invigorating, she thought, as liking yourself, and she did this day, though there were plenty of occasions when she didn't, much.

She was quite a useful citizen. She had that morning paid her rates, signed a petition to keep her town's old viaduct, bought a new blouse, washed and polished the car and now she was taking three venerable unmarried ladies on a glorious trip through the Peaks. Soon they would stop in the little town of Perry-in-the-Wood where there were two churches and a tea room that would provide china cups and scones with jam. By seven tonight she would have earned that gin and tonic for once and an hour in front of the telly, watching a soap if she felt like it.

In the back of her mind, the only

discomfort, was the thought that she was virtually in the same boat as Florence, Una and Ernestine. They were all what she had once heard a beastly man on an arts programme describe as 'superfluous women'. When she had passed her fifty-fifth birthday, two days after Father died, she had known she would never marry now. Would not even want to, for she had seen marriage chiefly in terms of children, family. She had helped Father in the business as well as at home and on his death had agreed that the other directors would take over. She was well off, her money safely invested. She sat on the parish council, worked for charities connected with the aged, had her water-colours and embroidery and her reading, deeper and wider than anybody knew, and holidayed with Elizabeth Carter.

They were great friends. She told Elizabeth things no other living person had ever been made privy to, including how much she had hated Father's addiction to whisky and how she would never fail to regret being bullied by him into staying at home with him after Mother died. That had been the big mistake, but it had somehow been pre-ordained, she had not been able to fight the perception that her Father needed her, would disintegrate without her. And so. And so, here she was, dipping up and down the Peaks with Florence, Ernestine and Una. Superfluous, all of them.

She wondered what had happened to the old ladies, what set of circumstances had kept them single. The curiosity about other lives which her friend sometimes found nosey and tiresome but which kept the animation in face could not be satisfied, because Una and Joanna's Ernestine were past the stage of meaningful communication and Florence did not quite perhaps trust her, or needed to direct all her energies just to making the appropriate noises of appreciation. They were, of course, very old, as old as the century and in Ernestine's case, certainly, more so.

"Where shall we stop for tea?" Florence was seated next to her in the front of the car and was obviously coming out of her earlier fuss and lather and prepared to play her part in the outing.

"Perry-in-the-Wood," said Joanna. "Did

225

I not say so? I thought it would be interesting and not too busy and I know a splendid little tea-room."

In the back of the car, Ernestine rustled. Someone had mentioned tea. Una smiled, knowing some new diversion was afoot. She hoped there might be a stop and a lavatory.

"I was brought up there," said Florence. "Now isn't that a coincidence? I lived in Perry-in-the-Wood till I went away to be a teacher."

"Is that what you were?" said Joanna curiously. "A teacher?"

"What else?" said Florence and suddenly Joanna had a vision of scurries of chalky little girls turning their faces towards Florence's voice and Florence's undoubted authority. (How much harder, then, to be on the receiving end of do's and don'ts, of Matron's good-natured chivvying and half-baked little nurses telling you when to wash your hair and where to hang your face-cloth.)

"I was someone to be reckoned with," said Florence, leaving no room for doubt. "They toed the line with me in those days — or else."

"How long since you've been back here?" asked Joanna, backing the little car into the cramped parking bay near to the selected tea-room in Perry-in-the-Wood. They were just on the edge of the town and could peer down on gentle streets of grey houses, the villas and semis of yesteryear, interspersed with the harsher brick of more recent building.

"Many a year." Florence stood on the pavement, trying to get her bearing. Opposite was a grey church mottled with lichen and damp and surrounded by spotted laurel. A peeling board set out the various Sunday services. "It hasn't changed much," Florence decided arbitrarily. "Nothing happened then and from the look of it, nothing much has happened since."

Joanna took Florence's arm and they made their stately way into the tea-room while the wrinkled marmoset faces of the other two watched them from the car. Florence walked like someone who was likely to get the proper hang of it any minute, stumbling over the threshold, blinking in the cool dank of the establishment's entry lobby. The tea-room, oak-beamed and soon to be festooned with white roses and purple clematis, did not open in the winter and still smelled of must and closing-down, and even now only opened its doors when the proprietrix felt like it. She was in it more for the interest than the money. But the tablecloths were freshly laundered, there were pictures on the walls and bluebells prettily arranged in white vases.

A rosy middle-aged face peered through the serving-hatch from the kitchen, announcing that they were the first today and a good thing too as it was baking day, the scones still hot and the sponges to be vouched for.

Joanna settled Florence at a table for four near the window.

"Two more to come," she called to the proprietrix, miming a patient face to show it would be a fairly slow process.

"Toilets," said Una urgently as Joanna coaxed her second passenger's unco-operative frame from the back of the car. With Una hissing uncertainly and crossing her feet they made for the Ladies at the back. The strain had left Una's face when she reappeared and glad though she was of Joanna's supporting arm she could almost have managed without it. Once she was installed next to Florence, Joanna returned to the car for the third passenger. Ernestine had almost reached the point of no return. One of these days, Joanna thought, that will be it. But somehow there was just enough response to get her aged guest from the car and from somewhere in the huddled heap of skin and bones enough courage to go forward. Joanna had half-lifted her tiny protegé over the doorstep and was thankful for the momentary gleam of greed in Ernestine's eye as she spotted the warm scones and jam being carried to the table. "Tea," said Joanna encouragingly, tucking a paper napkin under Ernestine's chin.

"You have picked the best possible day, ladies," said the proprietrix, bearing sponge cake bleeding red jam and soft butter icing, little crispy Eccles cakes, Bakewell tart glazed with a delicate icing towards the tea and milk already set out. "Now who is going to be mother?"

Joanna gave her a slightly frosty look. Who did it look like would be mother? The woman was well-meaning but baking-day must have softened her brain. Assertively Joanna put milk in the others' cups, pouring the tea carefully and ritually, making it clear she was in charge. It might be petty of her but she wasn't ready to be classed with the ancients just yet.

Florence had taken all of this in, Joanna realised as she passed round the scones. Florence might tire easily but there was a remorseless sardonic gleam going on behind those sharp eyes and a slight sardonic tilt to that long, mobile mouth. Joanna decided to let Florence butter her own scone. She spread and cut for the other two. Ernestine despatched hers with unseemly haste, the crumbs sticking to the long, stiff hairs that grew tusk-like down from the sides of her chomping mouth, while Una ate more slowly, taking in the pictures on the walls, the flowers, the young family who had followed in from the car park, enjoying the change of scene, being part of it.

A three-year-old child detached himself from the nearby table and came over, jammy-mouthed, to study the old ladies.

Curly-haired, sturdy-limbed, he was used to being spoken to and fussed over. The old ladies regarded him uncertainly, like a species from another planet. Mouth drooping, he returned to his own table where he launched into a tantrum over a chocolate biscuit. Joanna said, "Well, girls, if we're ready — " and reversed the earlier pantomime, getting her charges back into the car one by one.

"Have you seen enough of the town?" she asked Florence. "Are there any old haunts you'd like to revisit, while we're here?" The other two gazed at Florence hopefully, as at a bright child who will prolong the treat.

"Alderton Street," said the old lady. "Where I was born." They drove into the centre of the little town and there in a cobbled side-street found the flat-fronted, gentrified cottage where Florence had first seen the light of day.

"I remember oil lamps," said Florence, "and tapioca pudding. And hot salt put in a sock when you had a sore throat." Joanna gazed at her encouragingly. "I'm sorry," she added, "about the only other thing I remember is going down to the lavatory at the foot of the garden in the rain and the big rhubarb leaves tickling your legs." Ernestine began to chuckle and wheeze. "Rhubarb," she said. "Rhubarb pie." And then she began to cough and choke with such ferocity that Joanna became concerned. She wiped the tears that appeared at the corners of the old lady's eyes and offered her a black Rowntrees' gum she fortuitously found in her jacket pocket. Ernestine sucked on the gum with gusto. "Rhubarb," she said merrily. "Rhubarb pie."

"I had to black his boots for him," said Florence, looking back at the house of her birth. "My Dad's. And run the brush round the brim of his bowler. My mother sent me down to the corner shop there — " they looked out at Quicksmart Super Stores — "for headache powders and black lead for the stove. On Sundays we had boiled ham and tipsy cake."

Florence's face had grown pink and moist as the memories came back. They arrived thick and fast now, some illuminating, some banal, but in such a torrent Joanna cast around for a graceful way of shutting Florence up. They were

232

into family relationships now, sisters who had got out of doing their share of the housework, brothers unfairly spoiled.

"Would you like to buy a postcard or two?" Joanna felt her suggestion was a master-stroke. She pulled neatly up outside the post office in the main street. "You could pin them up in your room."

She bought ice-cream cones for the two old ladies left in the car and she and Florence chose postcards and inspected the few other shops that represented the hub of Perry-in-the-Wood. These were a so-called antique shop selling faded brass and grubby old books and toys, a delicatessen with curling ham and venerable cheeses, a Ladies' Outfitters with one spotted navy dress, a faded T-shirt and a packet of Tampax in the window and a Fast Food and Bar-B-Q selling kebabs and chips for the youths on their way to the Leisure Centre.

They came upon the War Memorial almost by chance. There were begonias and lobelia round its edge and in the middle a fading poppy wreath from last year's Remembrance Service.

Joanna felt a hand on her arm.

Florence said, "His name will be on there."

"Whose?" she demanded.

But Florence appeared not to hear her. She was away, no longer tentative of step, but eager. Her finger traced the names on the obelisk — "Anderson, Beltrane, Figgison . . . There it is!" Florence turned an illuminated countenance towards Joanna. "Garrow. Albert Thomas. That was him. Died at Ypres, when he was twenty-one years old. He had the nicest smile of anyone I've ever known. He named me his next of kin. I was the one who got the telegram."

Superfluous women! The phrase came back unbidden to Joanna's mind. There had been two million of them, she had read somewhere recently, after the war that had killed poor Albert Thomas Garrow.

She suddenly found she could not look at Florence's face. She knew it would be a face too naked and forsaken.

The shadows were beginning to lengthen and even in her cosy jacket she began to feel a chill. She should suggest to Florence it really was time they all got back to the Chase. Matron was a stickler for schedules.

But somehow she found herself rooted to the spot, prepared to give Florence all the time she wanted. In the quiet village street it was as though she could hear the guns of Ypres and Gallipoli crash about her ears.

When a youth passed her, going to the Leisure Centre for a swim, his T-shirt bearing the name of an ancient pop group called the Grateful Dead, she missed the irony but smiled kindly at his young and spotty face without quite knowing why.

TO FIGHT THE WILD
Rod Ansell and Rachel Percy

Lost in uncharted Australian bush, Rod Ansell survived by hunting and trapping wild animals, improvising shelter and using all the bushman's skills he knew.

COROMANDEL
Pat Barr

India in the 1830s is a hot, uncomfortable place, where the East India Company still rules. Amelia and her new husband find themselves caught up in the animosities which seethe between the old order and the new.

THE SMALL PARTY
Lillian Beckwith

A frightening journey to safety begins for Ruth and her small party as their island is caught up in the dangers of armed insurrection.

THE WILDERNESS WALK
Sheila Bishop

Stifling unpleasant memories of a misbegotten romance in Cleave with Lord Francis Aubrey, Lavinia goes on holiday there with her sister. The two women are thrust into a romantic intrigue involving none other than Lord Francis.

THE RELUCTANT GUEST
Rosalind Brett

Ann Calvert went to spend a month on a South African farm with Theo Borland and his sister. They both proved to be different from her first idea of them, and there was Storr Peterson — the most disturbing man she had ever met.

ONE ENCHANTED SUMMER
Anne Tedlock Brooks

A tale of mystery and romance and a girl who found both during one enchanted summer.

CLOUD OVER MALVERTON
Nancy Buckingham

Dulcie soon realises that something is seriously wrong at Malverton, and when violence strikes she is horrified to find herself under suspicion of murder.

AFTER THOUGHTS
Max Bygraves

The Cockney entertainer tells stories of his East End childhood, of his RAF days, and his post-war showbusiness successes and friendships with fellow comedians.

MOONLIGHT AND MARCH ROSES
D. Y. Cameron

Lynn's search to trace a missing girl takes her to Spain, where she meets Clive Hendon. While untangling the situation, she untangles her emotions and decides on her own future.

NURSE ALICE IN LOVE
Theresa Charles

Accepting the post of nurse to little Fernie Sherrod, Alice Everton could not guess at the romance, suspense and danger which lay ahead at the Sherrod's isolated estate.

POIROT INVESTIGATES
Agatha Christie

Two things bind these eleven stories together — the brilliance and uncanny skill of the diminutive Belgian detective, and the stupidity of his Watson-like partner, Captain Hastings.

LET LOOSE THE TIGERS
Josephine Cox

Queenie promised to find the long-lost son of the frail, elderly murderess, Hannah Jason. But her enquiries threatened to unlock the cage where crucial secrets had long been held captive.

THE TWILIGHT MAN
Frank Gruber

Jim Rand lives alone in the California desert awaiting death. Into his hermit existence comes a teenage girl who blows both his past and his brief future wide open.

DOG IN THE DARK
Gerald Hammond

Jim Cunningham breeds and trains gun dogs, and his antagonism towards the devotees of show spaniels earns him many enemies. So when one of them is found murdered, the police are on his doorstep within hours.

THE RED KNIGHT
Geoffrey Moxon

When he finds himself a pawn on the chessboard of international espionage with his family in constant danger, Guy Trent becomes embroiled in moves and countermoves which may mean life or death for Western scientists.

TIGER TIGER
Frank Ryan

A young man involved in drugs is found murdered. This is the first event which will draw Detective Inspector Sandy Woodings into a whirlpool of murder and deceit.

CAROLINE MINUSCULE
Andrew Taylor

Caroline Minuscule, a medieval script, is the first clue to the whereabouts of a cache of diamonds. The search becomes a deadly kind of fairy story in which several murders have an other-worldly quality.

LONG CHAIN OF DEATH
Sarah Wolf

During the Second World War four American teenagers from the same town join the Army together. Forty-two years later, the son of one of the soldiers realises that someone is systematically wiping out the families of the four men.

THE LISTERDALE MYSTERY
Agatha Christie

Twelve short stories ranging from the light-hearted to the macabre, diverse mysteries ingeniously and plausibly contrived and convincingly unravelled.

TO BE LOVED
Lynne Collins

Andrew married the woman he had always loved despite the knowledge that Sarah married him for reasons of her own. So much heartache could have been avoided if only he had known how vital it was to be loved.

ACCUSED NURSE
Jane Converse

Paula found herself accused of a crime which could cost her her job, her nurse's reputation, and even the man she loved, unless the truth came to light.

CHATEAU OF FLOWERS
Margaret Rome

Alain, Comte de Treville needed a wife to look after him, and Fleur went into marriage on a business basis only, hoping that eventually he would come to trust and care for her.

CRISS-CROSS
Alan Scholefield

As her ex-husband had succeeded in kidnapping their young daughter once, Jane was determined to take her safely back to England. But all too soon Jane is caught up in a new web of intrigue.

DEAD BY MORNING
Dorothy Simpson

Leo Martindale's body was discovered outside the gates of his ancestral home. Is it, as Inspector Thanet begins to suspect, murder?

A GREAT DELIVERANCE
Elizabeth George

Into the web of old houses and secrets of Keldale Valley comes Scotland Yard Inspector Thomas Lynley and his assistant to solve a particularly savage murder.

'E' IS FOR EVIDENCE
Sue Grafton

Kinsey Millhone was bogged down on a warehouse fire claim. It came as something of a shock when she was accused of being on the take. She'd been set up. Now she had a new client — herself.

A FAMILY OUTING IN AFRICA
Charles Hampton and Janie Hampton

A tale of a young family's journey through Central Africa by bus, train, river boat, lorry, wooden bicycle and foot.

THE PLEASURES OF AGE
Robert Morley

The author, British stage and screen star, now eighty, is enjoying the pleasures of age. He has drawn on his experiences to write this witty, entertaining and informative book.

THE VINEGAR SEED
Maureen Peters

The first book in a trilogy which follows the exploits of two sisters who leave Ireland in 1861 to seek their fortune in England.

A VERY PAROCHIAL MURDER
John Wainwright

A mugging in the genteel seaside town turned to murder when the victim died. Then the body of a young tearaway is washed ashore and Detective Inspector Lyle is determined that a second killing will not go unpunished.

DEATH ON A HOT SUMMER NIGHT
Anne Infante

Micky Douglas is either accident-prone or someone is trying to kill him. He finds himself caught in a desperate race to save his ex-wife and others from a ruthless gang.

HOLD DOWN A SHADOW
Geoffrey Jenkins

Maluti Rider, with the help of four of the world's most wanted men, is determined to destroy the Katse Dam and release a killer flood.

THAT NICE MISS SMITH
Nigel Morland

A reconstruction and reassessment of the trial in 1857 of Madeleine Smith, who was acquitted by a verdict of Not Proven of poisoning her lover, Emile L'Angelier.